Mr. Mysterious & Company

On stage, Pa showed the glass and looked through the tin funnel. "Empty glass, empty funnel, fat chicken," he smiled. "Behold!"

He set the glass on the velvet-topped table with gold fringe. He nested the chicken on top of the funnel opening. Then he held the chicken and funnel over the glass.

"Madam Hen," he commanded. "A glass of milk for the gentleman, if you please."

There was a hush over the audience. The chicken looked around as if spoiling for a fight.

Not a drop of milk poured out of the funnel.

"Madam Hen," Pa repeated, "Do as I say."

Not a drop. The undertaker, who hadn't bothered to smile in twenty years, almost grinned.

"Madam Hen," Pa said angrily. "A glass of milk, if you please—or I will turn you into chicken soup."

Instantly, a long stream of milk poured out of the funnel and filled the glass to overflowing!

Mr. Mysterious & Company

by
Sid Fleischman

Illustrated by Eric von Schmidt

A Beech Tree Paperback Book
NEW YORK

The text type is Veljovic Book.

Library of Congress Cataloging in Publication Data
Fleischman, Sid, (date)
Mr. Mysterious & Company / by Sid Fleischman ; pictures by Eric von
Schmidt.
p. cm.
Summary: The adventures of a family of magicians traveling across
the western deserts and plains in the 1880s.
ISBN 0-688-14921-9 (trade). — ISBN 0-688-14922-7 (pbk.)
[1. Magic—Fiction. 2. Overland journeys to the Pacific—Fiction.] I.
Von Schmidt, Eric, ill. II. Title.
[PZ7.F5992Mr 1997] 96-41225 CIP AC

First Beech Tree Edition, 1997
Published by arrangement with the author
1 3 5 7 9 10 8 6 4 2

For
the real Jane
the real Paul
&
the real Anne

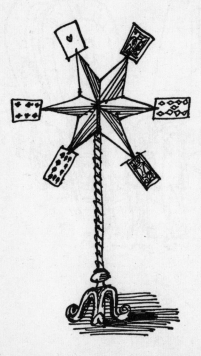

CHAPTER 1

It was a most remarkable sight. Even the hawks and buzzards sleeping in the blue Texas sky awoke in mid-air to glance down in wonder.

A covered wagon was lurching west along the barren trail to Cactus City, but it was like no other wagon seen in those parts before. To begin with, it was the wrong color. Its canvas was bright red and could be seen for miles. The wheels were painted gold, like a circus wagon, and the horses (if seeing was believing) were as white as swans.

The man driving this most remarkable wagon and these white horses was himself a most remarkable man. He wore a stovepipe hat, as tall as Abe Lincoln's and just as black, and had a smiling red beard even sharper than the letter V. If the hawks and buzzards could have read, they would have seen his name in golden letters a foot high on the sides of the wagon:

MR. MYSTERIOUS & COMPANY

The day was hot and the hour was noon. The gentleman (for even at this distance you could tell he was a gentleman) led the horses to the shade of a lone oak tree and pulled back on the leather reins.

"Whoa, Hocus," he said in a voice as deep as a bull fiddle. "Whoa, Pocus."

The horses looked so much alike it was difficult to tell one from the other. When strangers would ask Mr. Mysterious (who was a friendly man and always spoke to strangers) the secret of telling his white horses apart, a twinkle would come into his eye. A magician, as everyone knows, never explains his secrets, and Mr. Mysterious was a traveling magician. But in the matter of his horses there was no real secret to it at all. The animal on the left was Hocus and the one on the right was Pocus, unless they got mixed up, which sometimes happened. In that case, it was better to talk about the weather, which was hot everywhere that late summer in the year 1884.

The moment the wagon came to a halt, three young faces, in an assortment of ages from six to twelve, appeared in the puckered canvas opening behind the driver's seat. Two girls and a boy had been doing their school lessons farther back in the wagon.

"Are we almost in Cactus City, Pa?" the boy asked.

The gentleman lifted his hat and kissed them each in the order of their ages and said, "Be patient, young 'uns. We'll be in Cactus City by show time and in California by Christmas."

The children ranged in size like organ pipes, and they had the bluest eyes in any six counties. They climbed to the ground in their bare feet, and Jane, who was the oldest, smiled to herself. She enjoyed smiling to herself and sometimes practiced in Pa's shaving mirror. She wondered how she could wait both for Christmas and for the new life Pa had promised them in California. For the first time she would have a chance to make friends her own age, and keep them for more than a day at a time. Jane was almost twelve and beginning to consider herself a young lady, despite her bare feet. It seemed to her, during secret moments at Pa's shaving mirror, that she appeared very grown up when she smiled to herself. And one day Mama would let her wear her hair up like the older girls she saw.

"California," Paul grimaced, turning up his toes from the hot earth, which stung like bees. He was nine and wore a pair of Pa's suspenders cut down to size. "Shucks, who'd want to go to California?"

"Me," Anne said, clutching a rag doll which had long legs and a fixed smile. Anne longed to take dancing lessons when they reached California. She had never seen a real ballerina, but she had seen a picture of one on Pa's magic lantern slides. From that moment, she had begun to walk on her toes and to dream of satin dancing slippers. Everything seemed possible to her once they reached California.

"We might never get there," Paul said. At least every other day he changed his mind, and this was a day he

didn't want to go to California. "We might get stuck in the mud."

Jane cast an unworried glance over the trail ahead of them. "What mud?"

"It might rain."

"It might not."

"Well, we might get captured by Indians, then." Paul said that just to see his sister flinch. At that moment Mama, in her white sunbonnet, appeared at the wagon opening.

"Remind me to capture you before show time and give you a haircut," she said. "It's a wonder you can see three feet ahead of you with all that hair in your eyes."

Pa lifted her to the ground and she began to busy herself with the noon meal. Mama had once been a schoolteacher, and now she taught the youngsters their lessons as the wagon traveled from town to town. She also played the small portable piano inside the wagon and could sing all the Stephen Foster songs. "We're almost out of water, Andrew," she said.

"We'll get water and supplies in Cactus City," he nodded.

His name was not, as one might suppose, Andrew Mysterious. It was simply Andrew Perkins Hackett—which hardly sounded mysterious enough for a man who could pluck coins from the air and turn hens' eggs into silk handkerchiefs. He had, therefore, adopted a stage name, according to the custom among show folks. As Mr. Mysterious & Company, the family entertained settlers and pioneers in the small towns of the Old West, which at the time was Brand New.

The brightly painted show wagon carried all the tricks and props of their trade. It was full of lacquered boxes with trap doors and secret compartments, colored scarves, and silk ribbons. There were velvet tables with gold fringes, cabinets, and strange vases. Tucked in a corner was a hutch of white rabbits, waiting to be pulled out of hats. On occasion Mr. Mysterious had pulled rabbits out of ten-gallon cowboy hats, Mexican sombreros, coonskin caps, and even ladies' bonnets.

Pa printed up handbills on a small hand press. These were sent ahead to be posted on walls and fences to announce the show's arrival. Handbills had already been sent to Cactus City, where Mr. Mysterious & Company would present its show at seven o'clock sharp—unless the wagon got stuck in the mud. It hadn't got stuck in the mud since last February in Iowa.

"Let me make the sourdough biscuits, Mama," Jane said, adjusting the yellow ribbon in her hair. She looked rather plain in her dark calico dress, but on show nights she was able to wear her pink gingham and float through the air. She looked enchanting behind the footlights. Pa would pass a barrel hoop around her to prove there were no wires holding her up. It amazed everyone, except Jane herself, who quite naturally knew how the trick was done. Pa had sworn her to secrecy, and she had never told a soul. But then, she hardly knew a soul outside the members of her family.

"Do we have to have biscuits again?" Paul groaned. Jane had recently learned to make sourdough biscuits and it seemed as if the family ate them three times a day.

"Come along, my lad," Pa called. "We'll need to root up some wood for the fire."

Paul had already climbed onto the stilts he had patiently whittled out of old wagon boards. He practiced every time the wagon stopped, and sometimes he took his meals standing as long-legged as a young giraffe. The stilts made him almost as tall as Pa himself, but of course Paul didn't have a smiling red beard as sharp as the letter V. But one day he would, for he dreamed of becoming a magician like his father. Pa had already taught him to palm coins and small balls. He could untie knots in a rope with his toes. But it would take years of hard practice to master the difficult feats Pa did before the kerosene footlights.

Pa had brought along a shovel and began to dig for mesquite roots. "My lad," he smiled, "you can't dig roots from up there on stilts."

Reluctantly, Paul jumped back to earth and brushed the hair out of his eyes. He began hunting a mesquite root. Firewood was rarely found lying on the prairies and badlands. Wood was so hard to find that houses were often built of adobe or sod, and after a rain you could see new grass growing on the roofs. But there was mesquite to be found, and the roots made a good fire. Nothing else was at hand except Paul's stilts, and they didn't count.

"Pa," he said, pulling up a fat root and shaking the dirt out, "I wish we didn't have to go to California. Settle down, I mean."

"You'll like living on a cattle ranch," Pa said. "I grew up with cattle. Ranching is the only other trade I know."

"I'd rather travel around just the way we do. Seeing things and having adventures—why, we have adventures every day. Sometimes twice a day."

Pa shook his head. "The matter is settled, my lad. Your mother and I have talked it over from front to back and side to side. You young 'uns ought to have a regular house to grow up in and be getting a regular schooling."

"Mama's the best schoolteacher there is, I bet."

"No doubt about it," Pa said. He stepped on the shovel with his dusty boot. "But a show wagon is no place to get your schooling. No, my lad, we're going to homestead some land and raise beef, like your uncle Fred in San Diego. And your mother will have a house with a real kitchen and curtains on the windows. No two ways about it—this is going to be the last tour of Mr. Mysterious and Company."

Paul fell silent. He had to admit it might be exciting to live on a cattle ranch. There were some days when he thought he'd rather grow up to be a cowboy than a magician. A sheriff, maybe, or a U.S. marshal. But on show nights, with the footlights blazing up at Pa's face as he performed one miracle after another, there was no doubt in Paul's mind. He wanted to grow up just like Pa. He would rather be a magician than ten sheriffs. He wanted to keep traveling the countryside in the bright red wagon and never wanted to see California.

"Come Christmas," Pa said, "this family is going to settle down for good, like other folks."

There were times when Paul noticed a certain sadness come into his father's eyes at the thought of laying aside his magic wand. Pa loved entertaining folks and making them laugh, but once he made up his mind, it stayed made. "I hope Christmas never comes," Paul said under his breath.

He didn't really mean that. He liked Christmas as much as the Fourth of July and birthdays and Abracadabra Day. Sometimes he thought Abracadabra Day was the best holiday of all. It was listed in no almanac and printed in no calendar. It was a secret holiday that belonged to the show family. They had invented it, and no one else knew about it.

The secret was this: No matter how bad you were on Abracadabra Day or no matter what pranks you pulled, you would not be spanked or punished. It was the one day in the year, in the Hackett family at least, on which you were *supposed* to be bad.

As Pa had once explained it to them, "The way we live, moving about all the time, you young 'uns have got to be good. But no young 'uns ought to have to be good three hundred and sixty-five days in the year. So you each have one day to be bad."

There was only one rule about Abracadabra Day. You must not tell anybody the day you had chosen to be bad. The children sometimes planned for weeks or months just what prank they would pull on Abracadabra Day. No matter what it was, they couldn't be spanked, which was why they had named it Abracadabra Day. It was like magic to do something naughty and not get punished.

Paul was digging out another mesquite root when there came a shouting and a commotion behind them at the show wagon. He turned and saw Mama and Jane and Anne, all three, waving their arms like windmills.

"Andrew—come quick!" shouted Mama.

"Pa! Hurry!"

Pa dropped his shovel and whipped off his hat so he could run all the faster. Paul dropped a root and climbed on his stilts, but tripped over the shovel. To add to the confusion, it must be admitted at this point that horses and rabbits were not the only livestock traveling with Mr. Mysterious & Company. There was Madam Sweetpea. Madam Sweetpea didn't perform in the show; she tagged along behind. Madam Sweetpea was a black and white cow. Despite her name, there was nothing very sweet about Madam Sweetpea except the fresh milk she provided for the three Hackett youngsters. She was by nature proud, ornery, and the laziest cow north of the Rio Grande River (and south of the Rio Grande as well). She walked very slowly, and since she was tied to the rear of the show wagon by a rope, the wagon could never go any faster than Madam Sweetpea walked.

"Pa!" Jane said. "Look!"

"Calm down now. Look at what?"

"Behind the wagon," Mama exclaimed. "Madam Sweetpea! She's gone!"

"Vanished into thin air!" Jane added.

"The cow jumped over the moon," Anne said.

CHAPTER 2

Jane watched Pa tap the stovepipe hat firmly on his head and stride on his long legs to the rear of the show wagon. It was true: Madam Sweetpea was gone. Her rope was gone. The flies she switched with her tail were gone.

Even her hoofmarks had vanished from the earth.

"A splendid mystery," Pa mused. He stood sharpening the point of his beard and wondered how a full-grown, ornery cow could disappear into thin air.

"Pa, it's *impossible*," Jane said.

"Nothing is impossible, sister," Pa said. "Not if we put our minds to it."

Jane brushed a wisp of hair from her forehead and tried to put her mind to it. She knew that Pa needed mirrors or threads or trick boxes to make things disappear. But she had never seen a mirror or trick box large enough to hide a cow. And Madam Sweetpea, who weighed more than half a ton, could hardly have been plucked out of sight with threads.

"Andrew," Mama said gently. She was very worried.

"What are we going to do? Poor Madam Sweetpea. There'll be no milk for the children."

The doll in Anne's arms continued to smile. "Jane can't make biscuits now," Anne said. She was not smiling. She liked Jane's sourdough biscuits. It wouldn't be possible to make biscuits even with water. The water barrel was almost empty. The wagon had crossed a creek bed just five minutes before, on the other side of a small hill, but the creek was dry as dust.

"A splendid mystery," Pa said again, staring hard at the place where Madam Sweetpea should have been, but wasn't.

Even her fat shadow was gone.

"What's all the fuss?" Paul said, hurrying up on his stilts.

"Now that we have all assembled," Pa said, "let us get at the bottom of this mystery. Is anyone carrying a grudge against Madam Sweetpea?"

"She kicks," Jane said. "She kicked you when you weren't looking, Pa—just last Tuesday."

"How well I remember," Pa nodded with a look of pain and sorrow.

"She ate Mama's hat," Anne said. "Her Sunday-go-to-meeting hat. The one with the wax cherries on it."

"That cow will even eat rusty nails," Paul put in. "She's got no sense at all."

"Maybe so," Pa admitted. "Madam Sweetpea eats straw hats and rusty nails and kicks grown men. Those are ornery traits in a cow—or in a horse or a mule, for that matter. But she gives milk, and I suppose we'd better overlook her bad habits."

Jane glanced at Paul, and it seemed to her he was almost glad that now she wouldn't be able to make sourdough biscuits for the noon meal. But he wasn't old enough to make a cow disappear. He wasn't a magician, like Pa.

Pa lifted his hat to scratch his head. "Who last heard a sound from Madam Sweetpea?"

"She went *moo*," Anne said.

"When?"

"When we crossed the dry creek, Pa."

"Thank you, sister." A twinkle was coming into Pa's eye. "Then she was last heard about five minutes ago—just before she vanished into thin air."

"Pa!" Jane exploded. "Maybe Madam Sweetpea just ran away."

"But she was tied to the wagon. A good stout knot, too. I tied her myself."

All eyes suddenly turned to Paul, who remained on stilts and was casting a shadow as long as his father's. Paul, they knew, had been practicing untying knots with his toes.

"Young man," Pa said. "Did you untie Madam Sweetpea's rope as we were crossing the dry creek?"

Paul straightened his shoulders and said evenly, "Yes, Pa."

"So I couldn't make biscuits!" Jane said.

"In that case," Pa declared, "the mystery is solved.

Madam Sweetpea is just behind that small hill at the dry creek bed."

And at that moment they all heard a *moo* from the other side of the hill. It was Madam Sweetpea's voice, as loud and clear as a foghorn on the Mississippi River.

"Paul!" Mama said. "How could you do such a naughty thing?"

"You walk yourself behind the wagon there," Pa said, "and I'll administer a first-rate spanking."

Paul, who had kept a perfectly straight face, now burst out, "Abracadabra Day!" And then he began to laugh so hard he almost lost his balance high up on the stilts. "Abracadabra Day!"

There was a stunned silence from Pa and Mama and
Jane and Anne. He had taken them all by surprise.

"So that's what you've been up to, you rascal!" said
Pa, starting to laugh himself.

Mama forgot her anger and found herself joining in
the laughter. A moment later all five of them stood mer-
rily on the bare Texas badlands, laughing as hard as at
a circus—which woke the hawks and buzzards again as
they napped on the high winds in the sky.

"By gosh and by golly," Pa said. "I can't very well
give you a hiding on Abracadabra Day, so why don't
you and I go fetch Madam Sweetpea?"

They walked back over the hill, still chuckling, and

found the cow munching a tuft of buffalo grass. She was standing right over her shadow, switching flies with her tail, and her rope dragged in the dust. Paul, on his stilts, walked her back to the wagon—or rather, pulled and tugged on her rope, for she didn't want to leave the dry creek bed. He had planned his prank for more than a week. He had heard Pa call out that they would stop for the noon meal at the shade tree up ahead. That was when he had untied Madam Sweetpea with his toes. Now he had surprised them all—and he had even fooled Pa, for a moment or two at least. It had been like a magic trick.

After the noon meal Mama got out a soup bowl, put it on Paul's head, and trimmed his hair around it. Most of the boys on the frontier had their hair cut that way until they outgrew the bowl.

Finally, the family packed the cooking utensils and continued on the trail to Cactus City. If they got to town early enough, they would be able to visit the general store and buy all kinds of supplies and perhaps some candy.

The red covered wagon creaked and lumbered over the trail, and Madam Sweetpea walked along behind, with her rope well knotted to the tail gate. The family rode together on the wooden seat, watching the passing sights.

Most of the time they chuckled about Paul's Abracadabra Day. They would laugh many times, and even for years to come, over the day Paul made a cow disappear!

CHAPTER 3

Jane was the first to notice Cactus City off to the left of the trail. There was no sign pointing the way, but she could see the top of the church steeple. The town appeared sunk down in a small valley, as if hiding from sight.

"You children get back in the wagon and put on your shoes," said Mama. "We're not going to ride into town looking like a band of Gypsies."

Paul hated to wear shoes. With shoes on, he couldn't practice untying knots with his toes.

"Hurry Pa," Anne said. "So we can go to the general store before it comes show time."

She had been thinking of the candy jars for hours. Pa had promised them five cents' worth of candy each. That was more than a week ago, and her mouth had been watering ever since.

"Plenty of time," Pa said. He looked at his fine gold watch that chimed the hours. He was prouder of his watch than anything he owned. "Two hours yet before show time. I didn't figure we'd be getting to Cactus City this early. Plenty of time."

The trail forked off, and the wagon followed the dusty road leading down into the hidden valley. The family always felt an air of excitement as they rode into town. There were things to see and people to talk to and news to catch up on. And, of course, a show to give.

"Jane," Mama said. "Hand me my new sunbonnet. It's hanging right there over your head."

Jane unhooked the bonnet and handed it out to her mother. It was as white and stiff as starch could make it. Mama took a great deal of care to keep the girls' bonnets as crisp as her own. She made her own starch, either from the settlings of potato water or by soaking wheat and using the starchy dregs that settled to the bottom.

Jane brushed out her long hair and tied the ribbon freshly in place. Now that they were so near, she could hardly wait for Cactus City. There would be other girls, town girls. How wonderful it would be to live in a town, she thought, and carry her books to school and go to parties. She had never been to a real party in her life. She had never been to a taffy pull or a box social or even a sewing bee. The family had been on the move as long as she could remember. It was fun being part of a show wagon, but there were times when she felt a longing and a loneliness as hard to bear as a toothache. But now, with the rooftops already in view, a sparkle was in her eyes and her mood was light as a smile.

"Is my ribbon straight, Mama?" she asked.

"Straight as can be," Mama said, doing up Anne's shoes with a buttonhook.

Pa was knocking the dust off his trousers. "It wouldn't surprise me if they hadn't had a wagon show in here for a year at least," he said. "Maybe more. Everybody must be waiting for us."

"Looks like a pretty town," Mama smiled, tying the bonnet strings under her chin. "Joy! All freshly painted like it was born yesterday."

"Mighty quiet, though," Pa said, casting a glance along the main street.

The town was indeed neat and friendly and quiet as a clock that had run down. There was something strange about this town. Jane looked about, but there wasn't even a dog to be seen on the street or a horse hitched to a rail. Pa noticed that not a single handbill had been posted to announce the coming of the magic show. Not a man, woman, or child was on the board-walks to greet them.

There was not a soul to be seen anywhere.

The town stood empty.

Pa pulled up in front of the barbershop and looked around. "Mighty strange," he murmured. "A town without folks in it."

Paul gazed at the silent street. It was kind of spooky.

All the excitement Jane had felt a moment before was gone.

"Pa," Anne whispered. "I'm scared."

Mama held Anne a little closer, and Anne held her rag doll close enough to burst a seam.

"Andrew," Mama murmured, "where is everyone? It looks like the earth has swallowed them up."

"Look," Jane said quietly, trying not to sound scared. "There's fresh washing hanging on the line. Behind that green house."

Pa tapped the stovepipe hat firmly on his head and climbed to the ground. He left the wagon where it stood in the middle of the street. The sun was getting so low that the wagon seemed to cast a shadow from one end of town to the other. "You and the young 'uns wait there," he said. "I'll have a look around."

"I'll get your rifle, Pa," Paul said.

"Won't need it. It doesn't look like there's even a jackrabbit to shoot at around here."

Jane watched Pa cross to the boardwalk and try the door of the general store.

It was shut tight. Padlocked.

The children found themselves talking in whispers.

"Bet it's a ghost town," Paul said to Jane.

"I'm not afraid of ghosts."

"You are too."

"Well, how could there be ghosts in the daytime?"

Mama told them to get back inside the wagon, where they would feel safer. But even under the red canvas they talked in whispers. Finally Paul lifted the canvas so they could peek out. Pa was trying doors farther along the boardwalk.

"The whole town is padlocked," Jane said.

And Paul said, "Maybe everyone is hiding."

"Why?"

"They might be expecting an Indian attack."

Anne, whose heart was beating lickety-split, suddenly pointed toward Pa. "Look! There's an Indian!"

"Where!"

"I see him!" Paul said, forgetting to whisper. "Just behind Pa!"

Now Jane saw him too—an Indian brave, standing with full war bonnet, face painted, and a tomahawk raised in the air! "Pa!" she shouted. "Indian!"

"Behind you!" Paul cried.

Pa turned quickly and saw the warrior too. And then

the youngsters watched an amazing sight. Pa didn't duck and he didn't run. He merely stood there looking at the Indian, and the Indian stood looking at Pa. The children stood frozen, except Jane, who had shut her eyes.

"Pa!"

"The rifle, Mama!" Paul shouted.

But Mama didn't make a move. Couldn't she see what was happening? Paul wondered. He couldn't see too well himself, with the lowering sun full in their faces.

But then he saw Pa do a most remarkable thing. As if he had hypnotized the brave, Pa bit off the end of a fresh cigar and struck a match on the deadly tomahawk.

Jane couldn't stand it any longer. She opened her eyes and saw Pa blow a smoke ring in the Indian's face. Then he tipped his hat politely and walked away.

And the warrior just stood there as if frozen.

Mama (who had almost reached for the rifle when the children first began shouting) turned with a gentle smile. "You ninnies," she said. "Don't you know a wooden Indian when you see one? It's standing in front of the cigar store."

Jane let out her breath. She felt a little silly, but no sillier than Paul. Still, the sun *had* been in their eyes.

Pa crossed to the other side of the street and stood for a moment scratching his head.

"Look," Anne said again, pointing her finger.

"What do you see now?" Paul asked. He wasn't going to be fooled a second time. "Another wooden Indian?"

"A doggy. Under the sidewalk. See? Here, doggy."

Jane and Paul couldn't help looking, and there was indeed a dog hiding under the wooden boardwalk.

"Jump, doggy," Anne said, forgetting all about Indians. "Jump."

And right before their eyes, the dog, who was black and furry, with great laughing brown eyes, crept out into the sun and made a back-flip in the air.

"That dog's been trained," Jane said. She loved animals, whether they were trained or not. She lifted the canvas up high. "Jump. Jump here!"

And the dog jumped into the wagon.

"Mama!" Jane called. "We found a dog!"

Mama turned, her sudden smile framed in the white sunbonnet. "Joy! Why, the poor thing. He looks thirsty. His tongue is hanging out." Even though the

water barrel thumped empty, she added, "Jane, get the dipper and see if you can scrape him up a drink."

Jane scooped out a dipper of water and poured it into a tin pan. The dog lapped it up so fast the water seemed to disappear as if it were one of Pa's magic tricks.

"His master couldn't be very kind," Jane said, stroking his furry back, "letting him go thirsty this way."

"Maybe he doesn't have a master," Paul said.

"Then who taught him tricks?"

"Maybe his master disappeared, like everybody else in this town. Then we could keep him."

Pa returned from the far end of the street, taking long and merry strides as if marching in a parade. His eyes twinkled, and a smile lifted his eyebrows high up under his hatbrim. There was a slip of paper tucked in his hatband, and even Mama wondered what it could be as he mounted the wagon seat.

"Git up, Hocus! Git up, Pocus!"

"Andrew," Mama said, "what did you find out? You're smiling like a jack-o'-lantern."

"I'll put up in front of the bank, and you tell me what you see."

"What's that note under your hatband?"

"Git up."

The wagon creaked forward, and Madam Sweetpea protested with her foghorn voice. Half a block farther along, Pa pulled up on the reins.

"Paul," he said. "Read off the name on that bank window."

Paul shaded his eyes and read the gold lettering afire in the sun. "First Bank of Lone City, Texas."

"Lone City?" Jane exclaimed. "Pa, that bank is in the wrong town. This is Cactus City." She stopped suddenly. "Unless—"

"Exactly," Pa laughed. "*We're* in the wrong town. This isn't Cactus City at all. It's Lone City!"

And then he whipped out the note tucked in his hatband and read it. He had found it tucked up on the door of the feed store: *Gone to Cactus City to see the magic show.*

Mama took the note and read it again. "I declare," she smiled.

Pa snapped the reins and turned the wagon around in the middle of the main street. "Folks are waiting for us," he said. "They padlocked their town to see a magic show, and by gosh and by golly—we're going to give it to them."

"Git up, Madam Sweetpea," Anne said.

CHAPTER 4

Pa heard a dog bark.

"It must be a squeak in the wheels," he said. "We've got two horses, a cow, and six rabbits, but we don't have a dog."

"Yes we do!" Jane laughed, snapping her fingers at the dog farther back in the wagon. "And he can do tricks. Sit up!"

Pa turned and saw a black dog sitting up on Mama's trunk.

"Can we keep him, Pa?" Anne begged.

Pa stopped the wagon in front of the livery barn and the dog climbed into Jane's calico lap. Pa shook his head. "That's a fine-looking dog, but he belongs to someone here in Lone City. We can't take him with us." Pa climbed to the ground. "Hand him to me, sister."

Sadly, Jane handed down the dog. His tail started wagging, stirring up a breeze, and he began to lick Pa's face—red beard and all.

"Now don't you go trying to break our hearts," Pa said. "You can't come along. You belong here in Lone City. Now get along home."

Pa mounted the wagon seat once more, and the dog sat in the hot dust. His tail was still.

"Git up, Hocus. Git up, Pocus."

Pa was silent a long time. The young 'uns had always wanted a dog, he knew, but it would only be another mouth to feed. There was no place in the show for a dog. All the animals earned their keep; Hocus and Pocus pulled the wagon, Madam Sweetpea gave fresh milk, and the rabbits popped out of hats. A dog was just a dog.

Jane tried not to look back. No one said a word, and there wasn't a smile on even one of the five faces. The wagon creaked and swayed along the rutted trail, and finally a sign appeared:

Cactus City—One Mile

It was Mama who broke the silence, when she glanced behind to make sure Madam Sweetpea was still tied to the wagon.

"Look—he's following us," she exclaimed.

They all turned to look. The dog was indeed following in Madam Sweetpea's tracks.

Pa stopped the wagon and strode to the dog.

"Now see here, little dog. You don't belong to us. You go along home."

The black tail wagged a half circle in the dust.

"Hear me, little dog? You turn around and get home."

The tail stopped wagging. Pa took the reins once more, and the wagon lurched forward. But every time someone glanced behind, the black dog was there, following in Madam Sweetpea's tracks.

"He likes us," Jane said. "He wants to come along."

"Maybe he's trying to run away from home," Paul said.

"Andrew," Mama said. "His tongue is hanging out. All that walking in the sun and dust—he's thirsty again."

Pa leaned back on the reins once more. He sat a moment thinking hard, and the children held their breath. Then he tapped his hat firmly in place. "All right," he said. "There's no point in sending him home when we're so close to Cactus City now. Get him in the wagon. We'll find his owner and return him."

"Jump!" Anne shouted. "Jump, doggy!"

"Here!" Paul added.

"In the wagon!" Jane called out.

The dog leaped into their laps. Everyone was smiling again. The wagon moved on, and the children scraped another dipper of water out of the barrel.

The sun sat on the horizon like a huge pumpkin. The rooftops and false fronts of Cactus City stood on a mesa covered with cactus.

Much as the children had traveled, they had never seen so much cactus in one place in their lives. It was like driving the wagon through an enormous pincushion. Jane saw barrel cactus as big as nail kegs. Paul cast an eye over beavertail cactus by the dozens. Anne watched jumping cactus, hoping to see one jump. They didn't jump fast enough so that you couldn't get out of the way; in fact, Pa said they didn't really jump at all, but grew in leaps and bounds. Mama saw pancake cactus, which hardly looked good enough to eat, even with butter and molasses.

The whole town was waiting for the wagon show when Hocus and Pocus, lifting their white legs smartly, led the spinning gold wheels along the main street.

"There they are!" went up the shout. "Here comes Mr. Mysterious and Company!"

Pa lifted his stovepipe hat and the youngsters waved to the crowds along the boardwalks. The show wagon traveled the length of the main street. Folks in the hotel leaned out of the upstairs windows to watch. Boys and girls followed along the street (some of them doing cart wheels out of pure joy). They were dressed in their best calicos and homespuns. The ladies wore bustles and some of them carried parasols.

Pa halted the wagon across the very end of the main street and the townspeople gathered around. The show had been promised for seven o'clock sharp, which was just ten minutes away. There wouldn't be time to go to the general store—there wouldn't even be time for supper.

A man wearing a heavy silver watch chain across his ample vest stepped forward and raised his arm. The townsfolk quieted to a whisper.

"As mayor," he said, "I welcome you folks to Cactus City. Where's the show going to be?"

"In this very spot," Pa said. "With your permission, Mayor."

The mayor nodded. "Our young 'uns have been waiting all afternoon. We figured you got lost."

"We drove into Lone City by mistake."

"Don't stand there, jawin', Mayor!" someone shouted. "Let's get on with the show."

Pa pulled out his gold pocket watch. "My timepiece here says seven minutes to seven. We've been on the trail all day and we're a mite dusty. But our handbills promised you a magic show at seven o'clock sharp—and by gosh and by golly we'll give it to you!"

With only seven minutes to set up their props, the family had to work fast. Everyone had a job to do. Mama flew to the wooden trunk for their show costumes. Jane unpacked the colored silk scarves and flags her father would produce from "empty" vases and tin tubes. Paul set up the magician's table with the red velvet drape and the gold fringe. Anne brushed the lint off her father's black tail coat.

Pa rolled up a side piece of the canvas cover and let down a wooden side section of the wagon itself. It folded out like a table top to rest on two stout legs, and formed the stage. Then he lit the four kerosene footlights to be set out when the show started.

Inside the wagon a backdrop was hoisted and screens set up like stage wings. Jane changed into her pink gingham, and Paul buttoned up his blue assistant's uniform. Pa shifted Mama's portable piano behind one of the wings, and she took her place on the stool.

"All ready?" he whispered to his show company.

There was a nod all around, and Pa slipped into his tail coat. Everyone forgot about the black dog. In the rush and confusion he darted between Pa's legs and across the stage.

"Hey! That's my dog!"

A man shouldered his way forward. Anne peeked out and saw him first. Her heart began to race at the sight of him. He wore wide suspenders and a dirty hat, and his face whiskers stuck out like the quills of a porcupine.

"You there!" he shouted. "Come out here! You stole my dog Blue!"

Blue had disappeared behind the wagon drapes and was hidden, shaking and whining softly, behind a trick box.

Then the man climbed right up on the stage. Jane peeked out from one side and Paul from the other. The kerosene lamps lit up the man's face, and it was something fierce to see. The next thing Paul knew, the man had caught hold of his arm with a grip like a vise and yanked him out from behind the wings.

"You there!" the man growled. "You're nothing but a pack of rawhiders and thieves—even you young 'uns. Trying to make off with my dog!"

"Honest, mister—" Paul protested.

Pa strode out in his tail coat and stovepipe hat—and he looked even more angry than the stranger. "Take your hand off that boy," he said in a voice so sharp it could have split a rock.

The man turned, and his whiskers shook. "Where's my dog? Trying to hide him, were you?"

"Not a bit. He followed us with his tongue hanging out. He wouldn't turn around and go home. We figured his master would be here in Cactus City, so we let him come along. Sister, bring him out."

"Oh, you're not fooling Jeb Grimes," the man snapped. "I'm onto you actor folks. I'll get the sheriff and have you all thrown in jail!"

Jane picked up Blue and hugged him tight. There was a quick tear in her eye. She was sorry that he had to go home with the whiskered stranger. But she did what she was told. She set Blue at his master's feet. Almost at once the dog backed and growled.

"Come here, you lazy critter," Jeb Grimes said.

But Blue kept growling and then hid under Jane's long skirt.

Jeb Grimes faced Pa again. "You put a hex on my dog," he growled. "You turned him against me."

"No," said Pa. "Maybe you turned him against yourself. But he's yours and there's not much I can do. Now take that fine dog and get off this stage."

But Jeb Grimes planted his stout legs firmly where he stood and peered out at the townspeople. "Sheriff Johnson—you're out there, and you seen it for yourself. These show folks tried to steal my dog!"

The sheriff moved through the crowd. The star

pinned to his vest glinted like silver. He leaned his big hands on the edge of the makeshift stage. "Jeb, you've got your dog back," he said. "Now stop making a fuss. These people look to me like they're telling the truth. That dog of yours follows everyone but you."

"They had Blue in their possession, sheriff—and that's thieving."

"Maybe and maybe not," Pa said. Jane had never seen his eyes so narrow and hard. "Take off your hat, Mr. Grimes."

"What?"

"Remove your hat, sir."

"What in tarnation for?"

"You just said possession is thieving."

"Well, it is."

"Then do me the kindness to take off your headgear."

Jeb Grimes squinted and looked around him, and the sheriff said, "What are you afraid of, Jeb? You hiding all your gold pieces under your hat?"

"I'm a poor man," Jeb Grimes declared, and everyone laughed—the folks from Cactus City as well as Lone City. They all knew he hoarded every dollar that came his way.

Finally he took off his old and battered hat. Pa beat the dust out of it and then rolled up his right sleeve. Very slowly he reached his hand deep into Jeb Grimes's hat—and pulled out a live and kicking white rabbit!

The townspeople gaped in amazement. They were so startled they forgot to applaud.

But Pa didn't perform the trick for applause. He was still simmering with anger. "Now then, Jeb Grimes," he said, "what are you doing with my rabbit hidden in your hat? Sheriff—that's thieving!"

Now the audience burst into a roar of laughter and whistling. Everyone laughed but Jeb Grimes.

He grabbed back his hat and pulled it down almost to his ears. "Blue!" he shouted. "Come here, you ornery, ungrateful critter."

"Just a moment," Pa said. "Mr. Grimes, I'd like to buy your dog."

"He ain't for sale," Jeb Grimes said.

At that moment the watch in Pa's vest pocket struck the hour. It was show time.

Pa lifted out the watch, and the chimes sounded again and again—seven times. The chimes were clear and beautiful—as golden as the watch itself.

Jeb Grimes's eyes opened in wonder. He had never seen a chiming watch before. Pa had bought it in Kansas City.

"Blue ain't for sale," he said again. "But that's a mighty pretty gold watch you got there. Rings out like a church bell, don't it?"

"Get off the stage, Jeb Grimes!" someone yelled. "Let's have the show."

But Jeb Grimes didn't move. "Yes sir, a mighty fine watch." He scratched through his beard. "I'd like to have a watch like that, mister. You want my dog? I might trade for that watch of yours."

Pa closed his hand over the watch. He had saved a long time to buy it, and he needed a timepiece. There wasn't another watch like it within five hundred miles, and he didn't want to give it up. But then he glanced at Jane and Paul and Anne peeking out from the wings. And he could even see Blue sticking his muzzle out from under the hem of Mama's dress, where he was now hiding.

All their eyes were on him. A dog didn't belong in the show, and he ought to leave well enough alone.

"It's a trade!" Pa said firmly. He unclasped the watch from his chain and put it into Jeb Grimes's gnarled hand.

"Not just the watch," Jeb Grimes said. "The chain too. Or it ain't a bargain."

"Jeb Grimes," Pa declared. "You must have been raised on sour milk. Here, take the chain and get off this stage."

With that, he strung the chain loose from his fancy vest, which Mama had decorated with fine needlework. He dropped it into Jeb Grimes's waiting hand. Sorry as the children were to see Pa lose his watch and chain, it meant Blue would never again have to go home to Jeb Grimes.

"Blue!" Jane said. Her face lit up with sheer happiness. "Blue! You're ours!"

And Paul grinned, "You can come out now."

Blue crept out from under Mama's skirts and began to wag his tail once more. And Pa raised both arms to the audience.

"Folks!" he announced, and he was smiling again, "The show is about to begin! We present for your amusement, edification, and jollification our traveling temple of mysteries! A program of wonders and marvels for young and old! Feats of legerdemain and tricks of prestidigitation! Magic, mirth, and music!"

At this, Mama struck up a heavy chord on the small piano, and Paul, his buttons gleaming, hurried out with Pa's black wand.

"Folks!" Pa continued, with a gesture of the wand. "I present—MR. MYSTERIOUS AND COMPANY!"

CHAPTER 5

Jane was floating in the air.

Pa passed the barrel hoop from her head to her toes and back again.

"Behold!" he said.

The townspeople stared up in silent wonder at the small stage. Jane floated behind the footlights with her eyes closed as if she were sleeping in a magic trance. Her pink gingham had the enchanted look of gossamer. There was not a sound to be heard from the crowd. The men forgot to puff on their cigars and their eyes seemed as large as silver dollars. The children stared up in amazement and their eyes were at least as large as nickels.

"Is it real?" said Pa. "Can it be done? You see it before your eyes. A feat first performed by the magicians of China and India. Today it can be seen on the stages of London, Paris, New York—and Cactus City!"

Hardly an eye in Cactus City blinked.

"Now then, Sleeping Princess," Pa said very softly, "you will rise still higher."

And Jane, who was already floating three feet off the stage, rose another foot. She appeared as light as a feather. It seemed as if a sudden breeze would blow her away!

"Behold!"

The mayor hooked his thumbs in his vest and wondered if it was done with mirrors.

The sheriff hooked his thumbs in *his* vest and wondered if it was done with wires.

While Jane seemed to be in a mysterious sleep, like the fairy princess herself, the truth of the matter was that she was trying hard not to giggle. And Paul wasn't helping matters.

He was out of sight in the wings. "There's a fly on your nose," he whispered across the stage.

"And now, Sleeping Princess," Pa said, passing his black wand over her, "you will return to the enchanted sofa and awaken."

As if under the power of Pa's magic stick, she floated lower and lower to the velvet sofa on the stage. Even though she tried to put the fly out of her mind, she could almost feel it on the tip of her nose, and she had to fight back the giggles. It would have broken the spell, of course, but the harder she tried to keep from wrinkling her nose and bursting into giggles, the harder she had to clamp her teeth together. Paul! she thought. I'll get even with him!

Finally she settled onto the sofa like a gently falling leaf. "Rub my nose, Pa," she said in a desperate stage whisper. "It itches something terrible."

Pa, who had been standing with his eyes fixed on the audience, glanced down. "No wonder," he replied in a stage whisper. "There's a fly on your nose."

And at that she almost *did* giggle. Paul hadn't been teasing her at all!

Pa brushed the fly away with a pass of his wand, and then he clapped his hands.

"Awake, Sleeping Princess!"

Now she could open her eyes at last. She awoke and curtsied to the audience. Pa bowed deeply beside her. Then she ran off into the wings to a round of applause.

The moment she was out of sight she put her face in her hands—and giggled.

The show held the townspeople spellbound for well over an hour. It grew dark, and the footlights flickered. Pa made handkerchiefs disappear. He passed his wand over an egg, and it turned into a turnip. Paul, as the magician's assistant, showed a tin tube that looked as empty as a stovepipe, and Pa produced yards of ribbons from it. He changed red silks into green ones and green ones into yellow ones.

During many of the feats Mama created a mysterious atmosphere by playing softly at the piano. At the same time she was kept busy seeing to it that the youngsters got on and off the stage on cue, and she had to make sure the trick boxes and tubes were ready when Pa needed them. There was no time for Blue, who sat at Mama's feet and watched the goings on. But in whispers the youngsters had already decided between them to think of a new name for the dog.

"Mama," Anne whispered, "I'm hungry. My doll's hungry too."

"In a moment, sister," Mama replied. She was playing dark and mysterious chords. "The show is almost over."

One miracle followed another, and all the time Pa sharpened his beard and smiled. He set up the magic lantern, while Paul and Jane blew out the footlights to make the stage dark. Then Pa projected still pictures on a white sheet, for the magic lantern was nothing more than a "picture show."

A photograph of President Chester A. Arthur shot up onto the sheet, and everyone applauded. The picture was dim, and it flickered badly, but no one minded. Magic lantern shows were very popular in the frontier towns, for they gave the settlers a look at famous people and faraway places.

The black lantern box smoked and sputtered. It smelled of kerosene. Pa put in a slide of a Mississippi steamboat, and it seemed as if one could almost hear its whistle blow. Then came Civil War scenes, including a picture of Abe Lincoln by the famous photographer Mathew Brady. Pa showed a slide of a large Napoleon cannon, which looked as if it were going to fire right down the main street of Cactus City. It scared the ladies and small children. Pa himself had been wounded at Gettysburg. The Civil War had ended nineteen years before, but one still saw men in bits and pieces of their old army uniforms, for nothing went to waste on the frontier. Wives had made their husbands trousers, and even shirts, from old army blankets.

Finally, Pa showed slides of the Niagara Falls and the pyramids of Egypt and London Bridge. "And now a special treat for you ladies," he said.

With that, he showed photographs he had made in Kansas City at a grand reception where women were dressed in the latest fashions from Paris.

The frontier women, in their plain calicos and sunbonnets, looked on with *Oh*'s and *Ah*'s. The slim-waisted ladies in the lantern pictures wore feathered hats and beribboned bustles. It was enough to make a ranch wife's mouth water—and it did. But the frontier ladies made quick mental notes of what they saw, and in the months to come they would attempt to make similar costumes for themselves. The show would provide man, woman, and child with something to talk about all through the winter. They would argue their opinions on how this trick was done, or that, but they could never be sure—and they might even discuss it till spring.

Anne watched for the slide showing a ballerina. On the tips of her toes, the dancer seemed to come to life in the swirl of her costume. Anne was enchanted. Sometimes for days on end she found herself walking on her toes. Perhaps, when the family settled on the ranch near San Diego, Mama would find her a dancing teacher.

"And now, my friends," Pa announced, as he relit the kerosene footlights, "our entertainment is at an end. The show is over. We don't sell tickets, and if you have a mind to you can turn around and go home without paying the price of admission. Some wagon shows give an entertainment and then sell soap or patent medicines. Well, sir, we're not in the soap business *or* the patent medicine business. All we've got to sell is good family entertainment—and you all look like good family people."

The crowd smiled at this, and Jane and Paul set two tambourines at the two corners of the stage.

"If you liked our traveling temple of mystification, education, and jollification," Pa went on, "the price you saw on our handbills was twenty-five cents for adults and a nickel each for children. If you didn't like the show it was free. I see some of you brought along barter instead of cash money, and we'll be happy to accept it. My family and I haven't had our supper, and that pie you're holding, madam, has been making our mouths water."

"It's wild plum," the woman said.

"Sara makes the best wild plum pie in Texas," the man beside her called out.

Mama struck up a Stephen Foster song on the piano. The townspeople, if one could judge from the rattle of money against the tambourines, had liked the show one and all. Soon the edge of the stage was piled with things to eat. Folks were used to trading what they had for what they needed or wanted. Not everyone had coin money to spend. Paul saw a watermelon that must have weighed twenty-five pounds, and he licked his lips. Jane had her eye on a basket of raspberries. Two pumpkins appeared; a dozen eggs, a jar of honey, almost a bushel of corn, a jug of sorghum molasses, turnips and potatoes, and several jars of preserved vegetables. The edge of the stage began to look like a county fair!

Meanwhile, Paul and Jane and Anne changed out of their show costumes. Mama packed things away carefully for the next performance. They were as busy *after* the show as they had been *before*. Jane had the silks and flags to fold and put away. Paul had the magic table to take apart, leg by leg, to allow more room in the wagon. Anne began carrying in the barter from the stage.

"Don't drop those eggs," Mama said. "We'll need them for breakfast."

Soon the crowd had gone and Pa blew out the footlights. He carried in the watermelon and found a place for it under the wagon seat. Mama filled her "grab box" with barter. It was nothing but a large tin cracker box where she kept the smaller food supplies, together with her silverware and frying pan. Tomorrow she would cut the pumpkins into strips and dry them for winter. They would make a nice Christmas pie, she said to herself.

Finally, Pa folded the small stage platform back into the side of the wagon and let down the red canvas.

Then he mounted the seat and drove the team to a clearing at the edge of town, where they would camp for the night.

"Paul," Mama said. "Get a bucket of water at the town pump and I'll start supper. You children are hungry."

"Hold on," Pa said, a smile breaking over his face. "This family is going to eat in the hotel restaurant tonight. We made twenty-two dollars and eighty cents. I just counted it. Hard money. We're going to celebrate!"

And celebrate they did—although Paul had to bring a pail of water from the pump just the same. Mama wasn't going to let her family show up at the hotel restaurant unless everyone was scrubbed up clean.

Pa ordered the six-course supper for everyone. They had left Blue to guard things at the wagon, and they spent the first two courses of the meal trying to decide on a new name for him.

They tried Trixie and Wags and Blackie and Tray and Spot (even though he didn't have spots) and Pal and Duke and sixteen other names. But nothing seemed just right.

"That dog needs a special name," Pa agreed. "He's smart as a professor. He's entitled to an educated name."

"That's it!" Jane almost shouted. *"Professor!"*

Even Paul's eyes lit up. He tried the name on his tongue. "Professor," he said. "Pro-fessor. Yup, that suits him just fine."

Anne liked it too, and that settled the matter. Then, between the second and third course, everyone fell quiet.

"Now don't you youngsters go feeling bad about my watch," Pa said. "A watch is only a thing made of springs and wheels and gears. It doesn't live and breathe. It can't shake hands with you or wag its tail when it's happy or lick your face. Most of all, a watch can't love you—but a dog can. No sir, we got a fine bargain."

They all felt better after Pa's speech.

The hotel restaurant was a grand place, with wax flowers on the tables and two large oil paintings in gold frames on the walls. They enjoyed just sitting there, listening to the peaceful ticking of the pendulum clock near the door. Pa told stories of his boyhood on an Illinois farm. He had apprenticed himself to a traveling magician—and had been traveling ever since.

Jane looked around, but all the girls her own age seemed to have vanished from the town.

They were finishing their dessert when the mayor stopped at their table.

"A mighty fine show," he beamed, hooking his thumbs in his vest. "Are you heading for Dry Creek?"

"We expect to play there a week from next Saturday," Pa said. "We'll be on our way in the morning."

"I've got a brother in Dry Creek," the mayor said. "Newt Hastings. You look him up and tell him I said to treat you folks right. He's the sheriff there."

It was past nine o'clock when the family returned to the wagon. Anne had fallen asleep, and Pa carried her against his shoulder.

The Professor (for they informed him of his new name at once) was waiting with his tongue hanging out and his tail wagging. Jane and Mama had brought him table scraps wrapped in a handkerchief, and he had his dinner while the youngsters got ready for bed. Jane and Anne shared the sofa that was used in the Sleeping Princess act. Pa had once laughed, "Our girls never walk in their sleep—but sometimes they float!" Paul slept nearby, rolled up in a down-filled quilt. Later, Mama and Pa would make up a bed out of blankets and a buffalo robe in the rear of the wagon.

"Paul," Jane said softly, while Pa was unhitching the horses. "Are you asleep yet?"

"'Course not."

"I wish there was some way of getting Pa's watch back. He was mighty proud of that watch."

"There's no way to get it back," Paul said. "It belongs to Jeb Grimes now—and he wouldn't give it up for anything."

"If we could make some money, maybe we could buy Pa another watch just like it."

"It would take a hundred years. Two hundred, maybe. It was all gold and everything."

"I know. But we've got to think of something," Jane added.

And they fell asleep, thinking.

CHAPTER
6

The sun came up hot and clear, as if it had been cut out of a prairie fire with a pair of scissors. Pa was already setting up his hand press. He would print up handbills for Dry Creek and other towns and send them ahead by stagecoach.

"Sister," Mama called to Jane. "Madam Sweetpea needs milking."

"I'm brushing my hair."

Jane seemed to spend hours brushing her long hair and still more hours wondering what it would be like to wear it pinned up on top like the older girls.

"I don't know a way in the world to make pancakes with a hairbrush," Mama called.

Mama wouldn't let Jane wear her hair on top. Jane was too young. A girl had to be fourteen or fifteen before her mother let her give up braids or a simple ribbon in back. It seemed to Jane, as she fetched the milk pail, that she would never reach fourteen or fifteen. Until then—braids.

"Brother," Mama called. "We need another bucket of water."

"I'm helping Pa print handbills." Paul wasn't exactly helping, but he *was* watching. The printing press, like anything mechanical, fascinated Paul.

"I can't make coffee with handbills," Mama said. "You run down to the pump and hurry back."

Paul climbed onto his stilts, unhooked the wooden bucket, and went loping down the main street as if to catch up with his own shadow.

Pa stopped to build the breakfast fire and then returned to his press. The handbills, still wet with ink, read:

ONE NIGHT ONLY!
DRY CREEK, TEXAS

MR. MYSTERIOUS & COMPANY
Wonders! Marvels! Magic!

☞ SEE ☜

The Sleeping Princess – She Floats in Mid-Air!

The Miser's Dream – Coins From Nowhere!

The Sphinx – He Talks!

The Doll House

MAGIC LANTERN PICTURES

An Evening of Amusement, Education & Jollification!

FUN FOR ALL!
BRING THE WHOLE FAMILY!
SATURDAY NIGHT

Adults 25 cents   Children 5 cents

After breakfast Pa would take the handbills to the Wells Fargo office. The stagecoach, due about noon, would carry them on to Dry Creek and points west. A stagecoach could cover forty or fifty miles in a day. The show wagon, with Madam Sweetpea at a slow walk behind, rarely traveled more than ten miles a day. The handbills would reach Dry Creek long before Mr. Mysterious & Company.

Mama was ready to start the coffee, but Paul hadn't yet returned with fresh water. "Now where can that scamp be?" she declared. "Sister, look out and see if he's coming."

Anne looked, but there was nothing to be seen on the main street but a few chickens. "Maybe he got lost, Mama," she said.

Jane had finished milking, and Mama started the pancake batter.

"How could anyone get lost in Cactus City," Jane said impatiently, "with only one street?"

Jane was anxious to be done with breakfast so they could go to the general store. She liked to look at all the bolts of calico and the ribbons and buttons and imagine herself dressed up like the ladies in Pa's magic lantern slides.

Suddenly Mama caught her breath. "Andrew!" she said. "Put down those eggs. You'll break them!"

Pa had taken up the breakfast eggs and was juggling three of them in the air. "I've got to keep my fingers in practice," he laughed. "It's not often a man gets to practice with fresh hen-fruit."

"Put them down!"

Pa tossed one egg behind his back. It went up over his head. Mama stood breathless. Just before the egg hit the ground he caught it in his hat.

Anne applauded.

Mama breathed again. Sometimes being married to a magician was a trial. Once she had caught Pa juggling three of her best china plates, which she used only on Sundays. It was a wonder, she thought, that he didn't try to juggle their three youngsters!

Mama put the three eggs in her apron pocket for safe-keeping and poured out the flapjack batter. The griddle was sizzling hot, and the pancakes turned golden. "Jane," she said, "you'd better go fetch your brother."

"Here he comes now," Pa said. "And he's running like a swarm of bees were after him."

Paul, high on his stilts, came sprinting toward the wagon like a long-legged goose. Chickens in the street scattered before him.

"Pa!" he shouted, the water sloshing in the bucket as he loped along. "Pa!"

One of the stilts plunged into a gopher hole. Paul took a tumble, and the water bucket went rolling in the dust.

"Jack fell down and broke his crown," Anne laughed.

"Pa!" Paul yelled.

"Something's wrong," Mama said.

Paul gathered up his stilts and ran the rest of the way on his bare feet. When he arrived at the wagon he was panting so hard he could scarcely talk.

"What is it?" Pa said. "What happened?"

"I was pumping water," Paul started. "And—"

"Now catch your breath and tell us what happened," Mama said.

"And the pump's right next to the sheriff's office. And—and—"

"And *what*?" Jane asked.

"And I heard them talking. Him and the mayor. And—and—"

"My lad, if we could turn your *and*'s into steers we'd have a whole herd by now."

"Well, they were talking. About what happened last night."

"Well, what *did* happen last night?" Pa demanded.

Suddenly Mama remembered the flapjacks and turned them just in time.

"Well," Paul panted, "they were talking about Jeb Grimes. The sheriff is going to get up a posse!"

"For Jeb Grimes?"

"No," Paul said. "Jeb Grimes was driving his wagon back to Lone City last night and—"

"Get to the point, lad."

"Well, he came around a bend and there was a man waiting. With a handkerchief around his face. And he held Jeb Grimes up! Quick as you please. Took everything he had. The sheriff said Jeb Grimes carried gold pieces in a sack around his neck and the bandit took them. And your chiming watch, Pa! We'll never get it back now!"

"Never mind my watch, boy. Do they know who did it?"

Paul nodded quickly. "The sheriff said it was the Badlands Kid! He's big and mean—meaner even than Jeb Grimes. The sheriff said he picks his teeth with a bowie knife and would as soon cut out your gizzard as look at you."

Pa shook his head sadly. "I'm right sorry about Jeb Grimes losing all his gold pieces," he said. "There's good in every man, even if it is hard to see at times."

But the flapjacks were going to burn on the griddle if everyone stood around talking any longer. Mama got busy with tin plates and poured off fresh milk into tin cups, and the family started breakfast. But when Mama reached for the three eggs in her apron pocket—they were gone!

She raised an eyebrow and looked at Pa. Pa was sharpening his beard. "Andrew," she said crisply, for she knew how Pa liked to play his magic tricks off the stage as well as on. "Andrew—you give me back those eggs. I know you've got them. You 'magicked' them out of my apron pocket."

"Why, I wouldn't do such a thing," Pa said blandly. "You must have mislaid them."

"Andrew," Mama said and she raised the other eyebrow. The children watched now with expectant smiles and forgot all about the Badlands Kid. Pa liked to tease Mama, but he always made her laugh in the end. "Andrew—when a hen goes to all the trouble of laying an egg, I'm not going to *mislay* it. Now, you hand them over this minute!"

Pa patted Madam Sweetpea on the rump. "Young 'uns," he said, "have you ever seen a cow lay eggs?"

"No, Pa," they answered together.

"Watch and behold!"

With that, Pa sat on the milking stool. He rolled up his sleeves and reached under Madam Sweetpea as if he were going to draw a squirt of milk.

But an egg fell into his hand instead.

Then a second.

Then the third!

Anne's eyes popped. Soon they were all laughing—even Mama. It was indeed a comical sight to see a cow "lay eggs"!

"Joy," Mama smiled, as she cracked the eggs into the frying pan. "The next thing I know you'll be telling us a chicken can give milk."

"I'm working on that one," Pa laughed.

The show wagon pulled up between the sheriff's office and the town pump. Paul worked the pump handle while his father emptied bucket after bucket into the water barrel strapped to the side of the wagon. But Paul's mind wasn't on his work.

The posse was forming right out in front of the sheriff's office. Paul counted eleven horses and riders. He wished he could go along. There might even be a reward for catching the outlaw!

Mama wondered whether it would be safe for the show wagon to leave Cactus City—what with an outlaw in the neighborhood. But Pa had his rifle if there was trouble. "And anyway," as he said, "that posse means business. They'll track him and catch him."

"I hope so," Jane said. She didn't like outlaws at all—especially if they picked their teeth with a bowie knife.

Pa went over to talk to the sheriff. A few moments later the posse lit out of town. There was a great rattle of hooves and a cloud of dust, and the posse was gone.

"The Badlands Kid must not amount to very much as an outlaw," Pa said when he returned. "There's not even a nickel reward on him."

Once the water barrel was full, Pa led the wagon across the street for the long-awaited visit to the general store. Pa gave the youngsters a nickel each to spend. Paul and Anne headed straight for the tall candy jars, filled with butter balls and licorice and rock candy. Jane made a beeline for the bolts of calico. The material sold for eight and a half cents a yard. Mama had promised to help Jane make a dress for herself, and Jane had already saved up more than a dollar. That would be enough for the material and the buttons and maybe a little lace for the cuffs and the neck.

But there was so much to look at that it was like a visit to the dime museum in Kansas City. Chairs hung from hooks on the ceiling, and there were harnesses and kerosene lamps by the dozens. There was a smell of coffee beans in the air. There were black potbellied stoves and Stetson hats and buggy whips. There was a keg of horseshoes in all sizes. There was no end of things to look at.

The storekeeper had a round, jolly face and mutton-chop whiskers as bushy as squirrel tails. Pa bought two sacks of grain for the animals, and Mama ordered a fifty-pound sack of flour and a fifty-pound sack of meal. She picked the sacks out carefully, for each was a different color with a different pattern of flowers. A flour sack was nothing to be thrown away when it was empty. One made shirts or blouses out of it—or even underwear.

"Poor Jeb," the storekeeper said. "He never would spend a penny on himself, and now it's gone. Of course, he's probably got more buried in his yard. I guess he's the richest man in these parts, though you wouldn't know it to look at him."

"How did he come by such a fine dog?" Pa asked.

"Help yourself to the crackers and cheese," the storekeeper said, lifting the wooden cover off the cracker barrel. "That dog belonged to his wife. She's dead now, rest her soul. Jeb kept the dog. There's some men that need a dog to kick, and Jeb's one of them. It keeps a man from kicking himself, and that's been Jeb's trouble for thirty years. Now that he's traded you folks his dog, maybe he'll finally have to give himself a right smart mulish kick."

Mama helped Jane pick out five yards of calico in a sky-blue color, a spool of blue thread, and a dozen mother-of-pearl buttons, all for less than sixty cents. Paul and Anne kept staring at the candy jars and kept changing their minds. Finally, Paul chose rock candy, Anne chose licorice, and Jane decided on the butter balls. The choices were important because the youngsters knew they would have to make their candy last for weeks to come.

The storekeeper helped Pa load the sacks of flour and meal and grain into the wagon. The family climbed up onto the seat, and the Professor stretched himself across Jane's lap. He wagged his tail in Paul's face and licked Anne's ear.

"Git up, Hocus," Pa said finally, cracking his whip in the air. "Git up, Pocus!"

And the show wagon, creaking under its load, rolled away along the main street. Madam Sweetpea tagged along behind and snapped her tail at a fly.

Pa reached for his pocket watch out of habit, to see what time it was. The watch was gone. Reaching for it was a habit he would have to break.

CHAPTER 7

The horizon stretched out as tight as a clothesline with the long day hanging out to dry. A cloud of dust was rising in the distance, and Pa figured that would be the posse on its way back to Cactus City. Two days had passed, and perhaps they had rounded up the outlaw.

School was under way inside the show wagon. The children sat with their slates on the buffalo rug while Mama assigned them arithmetic problems.

"Brother," Mama said, "if a man walked five miles to town and five miles back every Saturday for a year, how many miles would he have walked in a year?"

Paul set to work on the problem. He was quick at figures, but he wondered how the man knew it was exactly five miles. It was too far to measure with a yardstick. Perhaps he had measured it with a wagon wheel. A few weeks before, Pa had pointed out a rancher figuring a property line. The man had tied a handkerchief to a wagon wheel and then counted the number of times the handkerchief spun around.

Jane was doing long division. But her mind wasn't on it. If she went to a regular school she'd be in the sixth grade. And she wouldn't be the *only* student in her class as she was in the wagon school. There was no one to pass notes to, and there were no boys to tease her except Paul, and he didn't count. How thrilling it would be, once the family settled in California, to have a graduation day. There would be speeches and frilly white dresses and maybe even a band playing. But now she felt very much alone as the wagon jogged along, and she tried to concentrate on her long division.

Anne was scratching out a pig on her slate. The Professor had grown tired of school an hour before and climbed up beside Pa on the wagon seat.

"It looks like the posse heading this way," Pa called out.

"I'll make some coffee," Mama said, closing up the book in her hands. And then, with a smile, she added, "Noon recess."

The wagon headed for the shade of a stand of cottonwood trees. Jane cleaned off her slate with a small rag dipped in water. Paul spit on his slate and wiped it on his shirt sleeve. "School," he murmured. "I wish I could figure some way to play hooky."

"You can't," Jane said.

"I know it."

He had never once played hooky. If he did, the wagon school would leave him behind!

"When we get to California that's what I'm going to do," he said. "Play hooky. Every day, maybe."

With the dust cloud still a long way off, Mama hooked the coffeepot over the noon fire. Pa cut open the watermelon and Jane took the Professor exploring in the cottonwood trees. It felt good to stretch her legs and spit out watermelon seeds as she walked.

Jane often wandered off alone to think her private thoughts. Sometimes she would bring a book along and wish she could sit for hours, lost in the enchantment of *The Old Curiosity Shop* by Charles Dickens or *Romeo and Juliet* by William Shakespeare. Mama had only a few books, and Jane had read them over and over. But with the Professor at her heels she forgot her loneliness and sent a rock skipping for him to chase.

When she caught up with him, the Professor stopped suddenly, his tail lowered, and a growl rumbled in his throat.

"What do you see, Professor?" Jane asked. "Why, that's only an owl in the trees."

But it wasn't an owl that started the Professor barking. When Jane took a step forward she froze.

A man was sitting there.

She could see him clearly now, through the trees.

He sat on a fallen log, finishing up his noon meal. He was eating a strip of jerky—dried beef—which filled out one cheek like a wad of chewing tobacco. He had scowling, bloodshot eyes, as if he had been riding all night. His hat was black as chimney soot. His eyebrows shot up when he saw Jane, and the horse behind him whinnied at the Professor's barking.

"Howdy," the man said. "You lost or something, young 'un?"

Before Jane could answer, the man began to pick his teeth a bowie knife!

She froze all over again. "The Badlands Kid," she said under her breath.

Without a word, she turned and ran. Her heart was beating like a string of Fourth of July firecrackers. The Professor left a final bark in the air and followed Jane toward the wagon.

The posse had just pulled up, and Mama was filling coffee cups.

"That outlaw don't appear to be hiding around here," Sheriff Johnson said. "We stopped over at the

Angus place, and the only news around here is Mrs. Angus had her baby early this morning."

"Pa!" Jane shouted.

Mama whirled round in fright. "What is it, child?"

"The Badlands Kid!" Jane exclaimed, out of breath. "I just saw him! Hiding back in those trees!"

Paul almost choked on a mouthful of watermelon seeds.

The sheriff put down his tin cup. "Are you sure?"

"I saw him!" Jane declared.

The sheriff studied Jane for a moment and then turned to the posse. "Boys, come on."

Pa drew his Winchester from the rifle boot. "I'll join you, Sheriff."

The sheriff nodded. "Pete, you and Charlie and Jasper circle around back. The rest of you boys spread out. All right, let's go."

Mama hugged Anne to her skirt, and Jane held on to the Professor, who wanted to go with Pa. Paul wished he were old enough to join the posse—although Jane had said the Badlands Kid looked mighty scary.

They waited beside the wagon while the men disappeared in the trees. There wasn't a sound except the switching of Madam Sweetpea's tail.

Any moment, it seemed, there would come a burst of gunfire. The seconds fell away as silently as sand in an hourglass. Madam Sweetpea began to swish her tail like a pendulum. Still not a sound from the trees.

And then the men appeared, with the outlaw in

their midst. They wore long and solemn faces. Not a shot had been fired, but they had their man. The sheriff stopped the posse in front of Mama.

"Madam," he said, "is this the critter your daughter saw in the woods?"

Mama, still clutching Anne to her skirts, glanced at Jane. Jane nodded.

"He sure looks bloodthirsty, don't he?" the sheriff said.

"He does," Mama admitted.

At that, all the long faces broke into smiles, and a howl of laughter went up. Even the outlaw himself burst into guffaws.

"Madam," he said, "this sun-beat face of mine is enough to frighten me myself at times, but I beg your forgiveness." He bowed low to Jane. "I'm right sorry to disappoint your young 'un, but I'm not the Badlands Kid."

"It's only Doc Bradley," the sheriff said. "He was on his way back from delivering Mrs. Angus's baby this morning. Hasn't had any sleep all night, which is why he looks so mean and ornery!"

"But he was picking his teeth with a bowie knife," Jane protested. "Just like the Badlands Kid."

"Young 'un," the sheriff said, "if I had to arrest every bachelor in these parts who picks his teeth with a bowie knife, I could fill every jail from Texas to California."

"Doc," Pa said, putting away his rifle, "you sit down and have a cup of coffee with us."

"I'd be rightly obliged," the doctor replied. "This is quite an occasion. It's not every day I'm taken for a famous outlaw!"

Jane traded a glance with Paul and felt as silly as a goose, but no one really seemed to mind.

As Dr. Bradley said before he left the posse, there was nothing better to mix with a cup of coffee than sweet laughter.

CHAPTER 8

Every day the horizon looked the same. There seemed no end to Texas, especially when you jogged along at about ten miles a day. Jane wondered if they would ever cross the line into New Mexico Territory. Would Pa really get them to California in time for Christmas dinner with Uncle Fred and Aunt Emma?

The show wagon crossed the New Mexico line on Friday. And the horizon looked just as flat and empty as it had in Texas. There were greasewood and mesquite and humps of tumbleweed waiting for a wind to come up. Dry Creek lay somewhere ahead.

Pa wasn't thinking of Christmas dinner. He shook the reins and wondered how to make a chicken give milk. He had been thinking about it for days, and finally, with the sun lowering, his eyes lit up. He had it! He knew how it could be done. He might even perform it the next evening in Dry Creek.

The show family wasn't alone on the trail. They saw

cowboys herding cattle north. They met a traveling preacher and stopped to talk. When they made camp that evening, beside a trickle of running water, they were joined by another covered wagon family. Everyone said "Howdy" and made friends at once.

The father, who had green eyes and hair the color of Kansas wheat, was a wandering newspaperman. He carried a hand press and type cases in his wagon. "Our name's Keith," he said. "We're heading south to Bear Claw, to set up a newspaper."

Mr. Keith introduced his wife Ruth and their three daughters—Susan, Martha, and Ellen.

Jane glowed with delight. Martha, with two blond pigtails, was just Jane's age. Paul was disgusted. Ellen was his own age—but she was a girl. Susan was fifteen and wore her hair up. Jane could hardly keep her eyes off Susan.

There was another hour of sunlight left, and the youngsters used every moment of it. They couldn't go swimming in a trickle of water, but they did get their feet wet. They played blindman's bluff and drop the handkerchief. They ran three foot races to a cotton-wood stump and back.

Then, while the women were getting dinner ready, Mr. Keith took a surprise from his wagon.

A bicycle!

Jane and Paul and Anne had never seen anything more exciting. Bicycle riding had just become a popu-lar sport in the larger towns, but a two-wheeler was still

a rare sight in the small towns of the west. The front
wheel was almost as tall as a wagon wheel, and the rear
one wasn't much larger than a soup plate. Pa rode it to
the cottonwood stump and back, with the youngsters
waving him on as if he were a rodeo rider on a bucking
bronco. He almost lost his stovepipe hat, but finished
bravely, still holding onto both hat and handle bars.

Then Mr. Keith gave each youngster a ride. He held
them on, keeping the bicycle upright, for the round trip
to the cottonwood stump.

"Supper!" Mama called.

"Time to eat!" Mrs. Keith called.

The two families had shared the makings of dinner. It was, for one and all, a feast. There were ears of roasted corn, salt beef, two pans of corn bread, beans, canned oysters, fresh milk—and for dessert, plum pie, raspberries, and a slice of cheese.

The Professor dug up an old buffalo bone for *his* dessert.

"I can't say I've ever heard of Bear Claw, New Mexico," Pa said during dinner.

"No wonder," Mr. Keith smiled, salting an ear of corn. "Bear Claw won't really exist until we get there. I'm a town starter."

Then he explained that several ranchers in the area had decided to start a town. They had hired Mr. Keith to set up his printing press. "I'll print up the praises of Bear Claw," Mr. Keith said, "and the newspaper will be mailed out to Eastern folks, folks with a hankering to head out West and start a new life. I'll write about the fine climate of Bear Claw, the clear air, the grand future. And folks will come, one by one. Soon there'll be a church and then a schoolhouse and a general store, and more folks will come. And pretty soon, the town fathers will have themselves a real town with real people in it—and maybe a hundred years from now it'll be as big as Kansas City or St. Louis. Yes sir, it takes all kinds to settle a big, empty land like this—and sometimes there's a printing press out in front of the Conestoga wagons and the emigrants. Why, I've started up six or eight towns already with my hand press."

After dinner, after it was already dark except for the flickering of the campfire, Pa and Mr. Keith moved Mama's small portable piano to the ground.

"I haven't seen a piano in a month of Sundays!" Mr. Keith exclaimed. "Folks, let me at it."

He sat himself at Mama's piano stool, cleared his coattails, and sent notes chasing each other into the night air. He played in a grand manner.

"Everybody sing!" he demanded.

The youngsters joined their parents around the piano and raised their voices mightily in choruses of "Buckeye Jim," "Old Dan Tucker," "Nelly Bly," "Susannah," and "Old Folks at Home."

Another traveler joined them during the second time around on "Nelly Bly." Quick introductions were made. He wore a tin star and said he was a U.S. marshal out hunting the Badlands Kid.

"But I heard all the merriment," he said, "and if it's agreeable to you folks, I'll bed down by your campfire."

"There's plenty left to eat," Mrs. Keith smiled.

"I'll pour you some coffee," Mama added.

"And there's all the songs you can sing," Pa said.

The marshal was tall and lean, with polished boots and fine silver spurs. After a plate of salt beef and beans, he carried his coffee cup to the piano and burst into song. He had a ringing baritone voice.

Mr. Keith's fingers never tired. He seemed to find notes that had been hiding in the piano for years. He shook chords, like a fall of leaves, from the keyboard. But finally the younger voices gave out, the piano was lifted back into the show wagon, and Anne was put to bed.

The campfire was kept blazing. The marshal went to unsaddle his mare and the youngsters tagged along.

"When do you think you'll catch the Badlands Kid?" Paul asked.

"Tomorrow for sure."

"Golly," Martha said.

"I might be a lawman," Paul said, "unless I learn to be a magician like Pa."

The marshal took off his badge and pinned it on Paul's shirt. "Try it on for size, young fella."

Paul stuck out his chest. It was a glorious feeling—but it lasted only a moment. As the marshal lifted off the saddle and set it beside his bedroll for a pillow, Paul heard something. Jane heard something. They both heard the chiming of a watch, clear and sharp, from the marshal's shirt pocket!

It sounded exactly like Pa's watch striking the hour!

Jane and Paul exchanged a quick, startled glance.

Was it really Pa's watch they heard? Who was this stranger? Was he a U.S. marshal as he said—or the Badlands Kid?

Paul didn't dare move. A creepy feeling went up Jane's back. They wanted to run, but they only backed away.

The stranger looked up. "Don't run off with my tin star, young fella," he said.

"Y-y-yes, sir," Paul muttered in a cold sweat.

Paul reached up to unpin the badge, but his hands were trembling so hard he couldn't get it off. The man reached out with his long arms and unpinned the star himself.

"Good night, young 'uns," he said.

"Good night, sir."

"And time you were in bed," Mama said from the campfire a few feet away.

"You too," Mrs. Keith said to Susan, Martha, and Ellen, who couldn't make out why Jane and Paul were acting so strangely.

"But Mama," Jane whispered, for she didn't want the stranger to hear. "Mama—"

"No arguing, now. In bed."

Pa and Mr. Keith were exchanging stories, and neither Jane nor Paul could catch Pa's eye. They made all kinds of silent faces, for they didn't dare let the stranger know that they suspected him. Pa only looked up to say, "You scamps ate too much. You look ready to burst."

It was no use. There seemed nothing to do but say goodnight to the Keith children and retire to the wagon. Once under canvas and out of sight, Jane and Paul whispered to each other across Anne's sleeping figure.

"We'll stay awake," Jane said. "Then, as soon as Pa comes to bed, we'll tell him."

Paul agreed. It wouldn't be hard to stay awake. Who could sleep with the Badlands Kid close enough to hit with a bean shooter?

"He's probably just waiting to cut out everybody's gizzard," Paul breathed.

"Unless he isn't really the Badlands Kid," Jane said suddenly.

"But he has Pa's watch. I heard it!"

"Maybe it isn't really Pa's watch at all. But one just like it. Then everyone would only laugh at us. Just like they did before."

Paul nodded in the darkness of the wagon. The stranger *might* be a lawman after all.

But the more they whispered about it, the more uncertain they became. It *had* sounded like Pa's watch—just like it.

It seemed they waited for hours. Why didn't Pa come to bed? Was he going to sit up all night trading stories with Mr. Keith?

Later, Anne awoke as Pa and Mama came to bed. She turned and saw Paul curled up in his blanket. He was sleeping soundly. She turned to Jane.

Jane was fast asleep too.

CHAPTER 9

A wind came up in the night, scouring the landscape as if with a broom. When dawn broke, clumps of tumbleweed had gathered against the wheels of the show wagon like brittle cobwebs. The sounds of five people sleeping under the canvas wagon cover could be heard, if anyone at all was listening.

Paul awoke first. He sat bolt upright, as if triggered by a spring. He couldn't believe he had shut his eyes, even for a second—and yet the red canvas glowed with the light of morning.

"Jane!"

Her eyes popped wide open and she sat up too—so suddenly that Anne tumbled out of bed.

"We fell asleep!" Paul exclaimed.

"The Badlands Kid," Jane whispered, in sudden alarm. It was all the foot racing, she thought, and bicycle riding and song singing that had tired them out.

"What about the Badlands Kid?" Anne yawned, but Jane put a hand over her mouth.

"Sh-s-h—he'll hear you."

"We better tell Pa," Paul said.

They crawled to the rear of the wagon, Jane in her cotton nightgown and Paul in his nightshirt. Anne crept along too. "What's so secret—"

"Sh-h-h!"

They shook Pa awake. Before he could yawn, they began telling him about the chiming of the watch and their suspicions about the stranger. Pa listened to every word. He pursed his lips and frowned and then sharpened the point of his beard. "It sounded like my watch, did it?"

"Just like it," Jane said.

Mama awoke. "What's all this whispering? What's happened?"

Pa pulled on his boots. He walked forward on the wagon bed in his long nightshirt and got his rifle. "Now all of you stay put."

Then he left the wagon, and the family waited. A moment later Paul heard him cock the rifle, and Anne put her hands over her ears.

"Now what is all this?" Mama insisted.

Jane explained, and Mama turned white.

A moment later Pa reappeared at the wagon opening. "He's gone," Pa said, uncocking the rifle. "Pulled out in the night. He's long gone."

The Hacketts and the Keiths shared the same breakfast fire. They discussed the mysterious stranger. Was he really the outlaw, or had a U.S. marshal come into a chiming watch exactly like Pa's? At any rate, the man was gone and he had not harmed them. It was Paul's turn to milk Madam Sweetpea, but Susan and Martha and Ellen asked for turns, and Paul was very obliging. The girls giggled, and Madam Sweetpea turned her head as if she were looking for a straw hat to eat. After the cream had risen, Mama skimmed it off and poured it into the butter churn. Then Pa roped the churn to the side of the wagon. By the time they reached Dry Creek all the swaying and jiggling of the wagon would churn the cream to butter.

While the horses were put back in harness, the youngsters found time for a few rounds of jump rope. Martha's pigtails flew. Susan could jump rope blindfolded. The Professor watched these goings on with an anxious eye. Then, suddenly, he leaped into the game to try it for himself. He cleared the rope once, twice— but the third time around caught him with his feet flat on the ground. He slunk away as if disgraced.

"I've got it!" Jane said, her eyes brightening. "If we can teach the Professor to jump rope, maybe Pa will put him in the show."

"Will you, Pa?" Paul asked.

"That's a smart dog," Pa said. "But I've never heard of a dog jumping rope."

"We'll teach him," Anne said. She was walking around on her tiptoes again.

"You'll have to catch him first," Pa laughed, looking up from the harness. "He's gone off to hide."

They broke camp a few minutes later. The two families said their good-byes. Finally the Keith wagon, loaded with printing equipment, creaked and swayed to the south. Jane stood a long time waving to Martha. The two girls had become old friends in a matter of hours, and now they would probably never see one another again.

Pa took up the reins. "Everybody in?"

"Where's the Professor?" Anne asked.

Pa laughed. "I warned you. That dog doesn't want to jump rope. Brother, you better go fetch him."

Paul jumped down from the wagon and found the Professor digging a deep hole beside the cottonwood stump. "Come on, boy. We're leaving."

But the Professor wouldn't listen. He kept digging, until all that showed was his tail. Paul pulled him out, picked him up, and started back to the wagon. But the Professor leaped out of Paul's arms and returned to the hole as if it were full of buried buffalo bones.

"Pa, he won't come!"

"Get hold of him and don't let go. We can't wait all morning."

Paul tried again. He dragged the Professor out of his hole and sure enough, there was an old bone between his teeth. "Smart dog," Paul grinned. "You didn't want to leave it behind."

But something bright in the bottom of the hole caught Paul's glance. It looked like the oyster can from last night's supper. Was that what the Professor had smelled? Maybe, Paul thought, he had been trying to *bury* the bone in the soft earth and had sniffed the oyster scent further down. But how had the oyster can got way down there? Once more, like a greased pig, the Professor twisted out of Paul's hands to return to the hole. This time, Paul pulled up the can—and a dozen shimmering gold pieces poured out at his bare feet.

"Pa!"

Pa came running. There was no doubt about it now. It *was* the Badlands Kid who had spent the night around their campfire. And sometime during the night, he had buried Jeb Grimes's gold pieces in an oyster can.

Dry Creek was a small cattle town that leaned with the prevailing wind. The store fronts, the hitching posts, and even the shade tree in front of the livery barn stood at a slant. It was Saturday noon, and one by one the ranchers and their families were coming to town in buggies and spring wagons. Wheels and hooves lifted the summer's dust so that you could hardly see from one end of the main street to the other. There was a great coming and going on the boardwalks and a jingling of spurs. The cowboys were coming to town too, in their checked shirts, their neckerchiefs, and their Stetson hats.

"Joy," Mama said, clearing the air in front of her face with an embroidered handkerchief, "this town needs a good dusting."

"We'll have a fine crowd tonight," Pa smiled. "Nothing perks up a town like Saturday night."

They found a vacant lot for the show wagon

between the livery barn and the barbershop. The side of the barn was tacked with posters that read:

Re-Elect

NEWT HASTINGS

Sheriff of Dry Creek

"Howdy, Sheriff," Pa said. "When's the election?"

The sheriff, chewing a piece of straw, had wandered over to the show wagon even before Pa unhitched the horses. "About two weeks now," the sheriff said. He had a young, friendly grin and stood straight as an awning post. Paul, who was already out on stilts, was fond of sheriffs in all sizes and shapes, but this one was different. Sheriff Newt Hastings had a broken leg. It was bound up with splints, and he walked with a hickory stick. He tipped his hat politely to the ladies—to Mama and Jane and even Anne. Jane smiled to herself.

"Why, he's hardly more than a boy," Mama said softly.

Jane straightened her hair ribbon and hoped the sheriff would turn his grin on her again.

"My horse ran over a cut-bank and threw me," he was telling Pa, tapping his splint with the hickory stick. "And this broken leg is going to lose me the election. I can feel it in the wind."

"Folks can't put you out to pasture for a thing like that," Pa said. "Your leg'll heal."

"Maybe they can."

"Who's running against you?"

"My no-account deputy. He's out hunting the Badlands Kid right now. We haven't had many outlaws around here, and if my deputy brings the Kid in—folks will elect him for sure."

Jane began helping Mama hang out their show costumes to air and was listening to every word. How could he be expected to go out chasing outlaws with his leg in splints?

"Sheriff," Pa said, "I wish we could help you. The truth is the Badlands Kid spent the night around our campfire. When we realized who he was, he was already gone. But he can't be far."

"Then my deputy will pick up his trail for sure—though we don't know what the Badlands Kid looks like. He's new in these parts. The stage came through from Cactus City warning us about him. Jeb Grimes has put up a fifty-dollar reward."

Pa lifted his hat and scratched his head in pure surprise. "You mean Jeb Grimes is going to part with fifty dollars?"

"For information leading to the arrest of the Badlands Kid—as the saying goes. It's as good as in my deputy's pocket."

Paul's ears pricked up. He and Jane had let that reward money slip through their fingers. If only they hadn't fallen asleep.

Pa turned the oyster can of gold pieces over to the sheriff. "I guess Jeb is beginning to change his ways. These gold pieces are his. The Badlands Kid buried them for safekeeping, but the Professor here dug 'em up."

"I'll see Jeb gets 'em back," the sheriff said. "What time's your show?"

"Seven o'clock sharp."

"The whole town's waiting."

With that, he smiled and tipped his hat again to the ladies and walked off toward the sheriff's office. Jane watched him on his lame leg, and her heart went out to him. She hoped he wouldn't lose the election. She wished there was something they could do.

Pa took Madam Sweetpea into the livery barn for a new set of shoes, for even cows had to be shod when on the trail.

The blacksmith told Pa that Newt Hastings was planning to get married. "Got his heart set on Mary Jo Abbey," the blacksmith said. "She lives almost the other side of New Mexico. But if he loses the election, I guess he'll have to put the wedding off." The blacksmith gave a shake of his bushy head. "A man isn't apt to take himself a wife if he don't have a job."

Jane and Paul and Anne spent a good part of the afternoon trying to teach the Professor to jump rope. They raised so much dust that the dog changed color— from black to brown. But the youngsters' thoughts kept straying from the rope. Jane couldn't get the sheriff out of her mind. He had such a nice grin—even while chewing on a piece of straw—and such courteous ways. But really, she thought, he had hardly noticed her. If only she were five years older! It seemed to Jane that growing up was taking forever. She wished Pa could wave his magic wand and turn her into a grownup— even if just for one day. Then the sheriff wouldn't dismiss her with a polite tip of his hat!

Pa was busy with his new trick. He was going to make a chicken give milk during the show that night. He had bought a funnel at the hardware store, and now he got out his toolbox. He was careful that no one was watching over his shoulder as he tinkered with the funnel. Within an hour he was finished, and he smiled with satisfaction. Pa caught a chicken and tried it out, and the trick worked.

He reached for his watch—and remembered it was gone. He checked the sun instead. It would soon be show time.

"You young 'uns get cleaned up," he said. "And that goes for the dog as well."

They threw the Professor into a nearby horse trough, where he swam from one end to the other and changed back from brown to black.

CHAPTER 10

"Ladies and gentlemen," Pa smiled. "Gentlemen and ladies. Boys and girls, and girls and boys. We present for your amusement, edification, and jollification our traveling temple of mysteries! A program of wonders and marvels for young and old! Feats of legerdemain and tricks of prestidigitation! Behold! Magic, mirth, and music!"

The kerosene footlights were ablaze. Mama struck up a chord on the piano, and Pa, in his fancy vest, his frock coat, and his stovepipe hat, bowed low. He looked mysterious indeed. The Hackett youngsters, behind the wings of the small stage, knew every word of Pa's introductory speech by heart. It seemed to Paul that he had heard it at least a million times, and he had learned to recite the speech backwards. Under his breath, while waiting to walk on stage with Pa's magic wand, he muttered:

"Music and, mirth, magic. Behold! Prestidigitation of tricks and legerdemain of feats. Old and young for marvels and wonders of program a. Mysteries of temple traveling our jollification and, edification, amusement your for present we."

"Brother!" Mama whispered urgently from the other side of the stage.

Pa was waiting for his magic stick. Paul hurried from the wings and tripped on his left foot. The magic wand went flying. The crowd burst into a roar of laughter, and Paul's face turned as red and shiny as an apple. His store-bought shoes, he thought. They had tripped him. How could anyone walk without tripping in store-bought shoes!

Someone handed the wand up to Pa, and Paul retreated to the wings. He wished he could disappear in a puff of smoke. On most nights the show went smoothly, but some nights everything went wrong. Threads would break, secret panels would stick, or the bottom would fall out of trick boxes. The show family sensed at once that this was going to be a night of errors and disasters. But Pa didn't drop his smile for a moment. If an audience sensed that things were going wrong, it would end up in howls of laughter and hoots and catcalls.

The Saturday night crowd gathered in a thick crescent of faces around the wagon stage. Benches had been brought from the schoolhouse and arranged up front for the smaller youngsters. Some of the older ones brought along boxes to sit on; there were a few camp chairs for the ladies, and in the rear several cowboys sat on their horses to watch the entertainment. Twilight was darkening the town, knitting shadows together, and soon the first stars would appear.

Pa was thinking fast. He had to win the audience—convince folks, somehow, that the show was running smoothly. "I have the pleasure this evening," he was saying, polishing the magic wand on his coat sleeve, "of introducing a new and marvelous, baffling and never-before-seen feat of conjuring. For this experiment I will need an ostrich. Did anyone in the audience bring an ostrich with him?"

The crowd laughed, as they should, for everyone knew there wasn't an ostrich in the whole state of Texas.

"No?" said Pa. "Then may I borrow a peacock? A swan? A sea gull? A stork?"

"I can get you a chicken," the blacksmith called out. "How will that do?"

"That will have to do," Pa said, as if in disappointment. "Make it a hen."

While the blacksmith hurried away for a chicken, Pa addressed the audience again.

"Is there anyone here who has seen a hen give cow's milk?"

There was a chorus of No's.

"How about you, sir?" Pa asked, pointing to a thin man with a long, gloomy frown. He was the town barber and undertaker, and hadn't been known to crack a smile in twenty years.

"I never heard of such tomfoolery," the man answered in a crotchety voice. "A hen can't give milk. Everybody knows that."

"Will you accept a challenge, sir?"

"What challenge?"

"If I can make a hen give milk, will you drink it?"

"No, sir. I can't abide the stuff."

Pa smiled. "But if I can't make a hen give milk, you won't have to drink it."

"Go on, Clem," someone yelled. "Take him up on it."

The barber-undertaker shook his gloomy head. "I ain't drunk milk in forty-odd years," he said. "But you can't get anything but eggs from a hen. I'm onto your fakery. You got everything up your sleeves."

"If I roll up my sleeves?"

"Then it's a bargain. I'll drink the milk."

Pa rolled up his sleeves to the elbow, and the blacksmith returned with the hen. She was a big fat one, with red, flapping wings and a temper. Pa held her by the legs and called for his props. Paul had the funnel ready, but he hated to face the crowd. What if he tripped again? He stood in the wings, unable to move.

"Hurry, my lad."

There was a tone of command in Pa's voice, and Paul swallowed hard. Then he put one foot carefully in front of the other.

"Trip again," Pa whispered.

Paul could hardly believe his ears. Did Pa want to make him a laughingstock all over again?

"Do as I say."

Paul tripped. Tears all but sprang into his eyes as the crowd howled. Pa caught the funnel in mid-air.

"Thank you, my lad. Now if you will fetch a glass."

Paul returned to the wings for the glass and wanted to run clear away. He would become a cowboy. He didn't want to return to the show—to the stage—to Dry Creek. He looked around for Jane. Where was she? Why couldn't she bring Pa his glass?

But Jane wasn't in the wings, and Anne was across the stage with Mama at the piano. Paul picked up the glass. He took another breath and started on stage once more.

"Trip again," Pa whispered.

Paul fought back tears and tripped again. Pa caught the glass, and the crowd howled.

But picking himself up, Paul realized that the laughter had changed in tone. It had a good-natured sound. Folks had come to believe his clumsiness was part of the show! That was what Pa had in mind! What had begun as an embarrassing fall had been turned into entertainment. The audience loved it!

Paul returned to the wings smiling. Maybe, he thought suddenly, they ought to keep the comic falls in the show every night. That made him a kind of performer—almost like an acrobat. But where, he wondered, was Jane?

On stage, Pa showed the glass and looked through the tin funnel. "Empty glass, empty funnel, fat chicken," he smiled. "Behold!"

He set the glass on the velvet-topped table with gold fringe. He nested the chicken on top of the funnel opening. Then he held the chicken and funnel over the glass.

"Madam Hen," he commanded. "A glass of milk for the gentleman, if you please."

There was a hush over the audience. The chicken looked around as if spoiling for a fight.

Not a drop of milk poured out of the funnel.

"Madam Hen," Pa repeated, "Do as I say."

Not a drop. The undertaker, who hadn't bothered to smile in twenty years, almost grinned.

"Madam Hen," Pa said angrily. "A glass of milk, if you please—or I will turn you into chicken soup."

Instantly, a long stream of milk poured out of the funnel and filled the glass to overflowing!

The undertaker's gloomy face lengthened. The townsfolk roared. Sheriff Newt Hastings called out, "Clem—you promised to drink it!"

"But I ain't tasted the stuff in forty years!"

"You're about to now!"

Pa gave out the glass, which

was passed from hand to hand until it reached the undertaker.

"It's all yours, Clem!" a cowboy called out.

"But—"

"A man that don't stand by his word don't amount to much."

The undertaker smelled the milk and wrinkled up his thin nose. "I always stand by my word—but I can't stand the smell of milk."

"Then I'll hold your nose for you," a neighbor laughed.

With the neighbor's fingers clamped like a clothespin to his nose, the undertaker poured down the milk. The crowd watched, smiling all the while, and then applauded—for they were enjoying themselves. When the glass was almost empty the undertaker took a final gulp and lowered the glass, and a strange expression came over his face. He licked his lips. His eyes lit up. He grinned. Then he smiled!

Folks around him could hardly believe what they saw. A smile on their undertaker's face. And a large, toothy smile at that!

"I declare," the undertaker beamed. "Why—I declare. That stuff don't taste half bad. Reminds me of when I was a kid."

"Clem," said a gray-haired woman standing nearby, "you haven't cracked a smile since you were a kid either."

"But milk from a chicken—I never saw such a thing!"

Pa's new trick was a complete success. If the show had started out badly, Pa, using tactics like a general in battle, had won his audience. There would be no cat-calls now. The chicken trick had fooled them, but Pa had performed an even finer miracle. He had put a smile on the undertaker's face!

In the wings, Paul whispered urgently, "Jane!"

There came no answer. Jane seemed to have vanished—and Pa would be needing her in the very next trick.

CHAPTER 11

The footlights held Pa's wizard's face in a flickering glow. His voice was strong and deep. "Mystery of mysteries," he said. "The possible impossible. The impossible possible. The greatest feat of the ages. Suspension by sorcery. Levitation by magic. I present—the Sleeping Princess Illusion."

That was Jane's cue. He turned for her entrance.

But Jane didn't enter.

"I present," Pa said again, with a flashing glance at the wings—"the Sleeping Princess Illusion."

Jane wasn't at the wings. But there was a flutter behind the back curtain.

The curtains parted, and Jane appeared. She held her head high and avoided Pa's eyes. She had been hiding, as still as a stick of furniture. Her heart thumped. She had hesitated to show herself, but now it was too late to change her mind. Like Pa himself, once she made up her mind it stayed made.

"Sister," Pa breathed in a stage whisper. He was almost too stunned to go on with the trick. "What in tarnation have you done to your hair?"

"I put it up, Pa."

"I can see that."

Mama missed a chord on the piano and stared at Jane as if she were a stranger. Jane had pinned up her hair like the older girls. She looked fifteen. "Jane Hackett," Mama whispered across the stage. "Wait till I get my hands on you!"

With an audience on the other side of the footlights, Pa had to go on with the trick. There was no time now for a tongue-lashing.

Within moments, Jane was floating in mid-air. She could feel Sheriff Newt Hastings's eyes on her. In the pink gingham and with her hair up, she felt enchanted. She felt like a real sleeping princess. It was like a dream, and she would hate to come back to earth and be awakened. She would like to go on dreaming this way for twenty years.

Behind the wings, Anne turned to Mama. "I want my hair up—like Jane."

"Be still," Mama said. She had to admit that Jane looked lovely. But she didn't want to see her youngsters grow up too fast. "Next thing I know, she'll be wanting to wear a bustle."

"I want to wear a bustle too," Anne exclaimed.

"You'll both get a hiding."

Pa held his magic stick over Jane and commanded

her to descend. Soon her act would be over. She didn't want it to be over. What was the sheriff thinking? That she was mysterious and beautiful? She didn't want the sheriff to stop looking at her. She had read in books about young ladies swooning with love, and she wondered what *that* would be like.

"Awaken, Sleeping Princess," she heard Pa command in his deep voice.

But she didn't awaken. She refused to open her eyes. She felt like swooning. She would pretend she was swooning. "Awaken," Pa said again, clapping his hands over her eyes.

But Jane kept her eyes tightly shut.

"Wake up," Pa whispered.

"Abracadabra Day," Jane whispered back.

Pa stopped short. And then he couldn't help smiling to himself. "You rascal," he said under his breath.

She had declared a holiday and was determined to make the best of it. But Pa couldn't let her sleep on stage throughout the performance. He began to stroke the lapel of his coat, where he kept a straight pin on the underside, and before she knew it Jane felt a pinprick. Her eyes popped open—and the trick was over.

Applause thundered out over the show wagon. As she curtsied to the audience, she could see the sheriff clapping hardest of all. She felt entirely pleased with her special performance. She left the stage smiling and touched her hair as if to assure herself that it really was piled on top of her head.

"Abracadabra Day, Mama," Jane said in the wings.

"What—" Mama's anger gave way. "And I've been sitting here waiting to get my hands on that hair of yours."

Jane gave her mother a kiss. "I'll take it down after the show."

"I want my hair up," Anne protested.

"Girls," Mama said. She had only a moment, for Pa was beginning the next trick and she had background music to play. "I love you both dearly and enjoy seeing you happy and smiling. Pa does tricks to entertain folks. Putting your hair up to look older is only a trick too—but a different kind of trick. To deceive folks. Because, no matter what you do to yourself, you're still a twelve-year-old. Your hair can't change that. Only time can. If I was angry, it was because I don't like to see you deceive yourself as well. Why, it's wonderful to be twelve or five or sixteen or sixty. Every age is a wonderful age. Now go along with you."

In front of the footlights, one mystery followed another. As Pa expected, however, there was a second mishap. A thread broke when he was causing a finger ring to rise and fall on his wand. But he managed to cover his embarrassment by making the ring disappear entirely, and the audience was no wiser.

Pa was performing in front of a drawn stage curtain. Behind it, Paul was being readied for the Sphinx Illusion. Mama put on him a stringy black wig (it looked a fright—and was called, as you might expect, a fright wig) and then affixed a drooping mustache and beard with spirit gum. She marked lines on his face with a grease pencil. When she finished he looked two hundred years old—almost as old as the Sphinx himself.

A three-legged table was placed in center stage, and Paul, climbing into a secret place, disappeared from sight. One could see under the table—or so it seemed—but no one could see Paul, his fright wig, his mustache, or his beard.

"And now," Pa announced at the footlights. "The Great Sphinx—he talks, he knows all, he will answer three questions! Open the curtains, if you please."

Jane pulled the cords, and the front curtains parted. There was nothing to be seen on stage but the three-legged table, which stood in perfect innocence.

"And now," Pa exclaimed, with a clap of his hands, "bring out the Egyptian Box."

Anne, knowing her cue, hurried out with a wooden box, painted red and gold, and handed it to Pa. She was careful not to trip on the floor boards.

The Egyptian Box was a foot square. It had a front door that opened on brass hinges. Pa opened the door and showed everyone that the box was empty. Then he placed it on the table.

"And now, my friends—behold!"

After a pass of his magic stick, he opened the door—slowly. The hinges creaked and shivers went up a few backs.

"The Sphinx . . ." Pa announced.

The empty box was no longer empty. A face with dark eyes looked out of the box. It was a face that looked two hundred years old!

"A living head in a square box," Pa said. "It thinks, it speaks—it can wrinkle its nose."

Paul wrinkled his nose and twitched his mustache. Many folks who had taken the head in the box for a dummy now leaned closer. Where was the body? They could see under the table, but there was nothing to see—no shoes, no legs, no chest, no arms.

"Good evening, Sphinx," Pa said to the head in the box.

Paul, in reply, pitched his voice as low as he could. "Good evening, Mr. Mysterious."

"Will you answer three questions for these kind people?"

The Sphinx nodded his head, and Pa turned to the crowd.

"Who has a question for the Sphinx?"

"I do," called out a rancher. "Is the sheriff here going to get himself re-elected?"

Paul watched his father's hands for a signal and then answered. "Yes," he said deeply.

This prediction met with smiles and applause. Everyone liked Newt Hastings, but some had doubts about re-electing a sheriff who might be hobbling on a lame leg for another six months.

A lady called out, "Who stole four of my chickens?"

As the Sphinx, Paul was often asked about stolen

chickens, and he had learned a pat answer. "Coyotes," he declared.

And then Sheriff Hastings stepped closer. "Sphinx," he said. "Where's the Badlands Kid?"

There was a general titter over that question, for not even the wise Sphinx could be expected to answer it.

With his head in the box, Paul looked out at the footlights and the sea of heads beyond the stage. Everyone was looking at him—even Pa—and waiting for an answer. It was hot in the box, and his face was sweating. As his eyes scanned the youngsters on benches, the ladies on camp chairs, and the cowboys sitting their horses at the rear—his false eyebrows shot up. He saw a familiar face.

He saw the Badlands Kid himself!

"Well?" Pa asked. "What is your answer, Sphinx?" In a stage whisper, Pa added, "Say he's somewhere in Texas."

But Paul didn't say a word. The beat of his heart sounded as loud as a peckerwood. Was it really the Badlands Kid at the back of the crowd? Had the outlaw come to town—unable to resist watching the magic show? And sure he wouldn't be recognized?

"Sphinx," Pa said impatiently, "we're waiting for your answer."

"The Badlands Kid—" Paul hesitated. It *looked* like the outlaw, but with the footlights in his eyes Paul couldn't be sure. The man sat hunched over his saddle horn and was smiling as friendly as he could be. Paul peered as hard as he could.

And then he saw the flash of a marshal's badge on the horseman's vest.

It had to be the Badlands Kid!

Paul was sure of it now.

But if he said so out loud, there would be gunplay right in the crowd. Youngsters might get hurt and some of the ladies too.

Sweat poured down Paul's made-up face. His drooping mustache drooped still lower. He could feel the sweat trickling clear down into his shoes—even if no one could see his shoes.

"I'll whisper the answer in the sheriff's ear," he croaked at last.

Pa could tell that something was wrong.

"All right," he said. "Sheriff, step up here."

A box was placed near the edge of the stage, and Newt Hastings climbed up, broken leg and all. "I'm ready, Mr. Sphinx," he smiled.

"Lean closer," the Sphinx said.

The sheriff leaned closer.

"Closer than that," the Sphinx said.

The sheriff leaned his ear right in front of the Egyptian Box. And then the Sphinx whispered:

"There, Sheriff! Near the water trough. Sitting his horse. Look—he's picking his teeth with a bowie knife! That's him!"

The sheriff straightened. He looked around at the crowd and winked at the folks. "The Sphinx here says the Badlands Kid is back across the line in Texas. Boys, hand me my rope. As long as we're having an evening of tricks, I'd like to do a few rope stunts."

"Pa!" Jane whispered from the wings. "I see him! The Badlands Kid. He's out there!"

Aware now of what the sheriff was up to, Pa said, "I'll step aside for a good rope trick any time. Spin away, Sheriff."

The sheriff, despite his broken leg, got the lariat swirling over his head like an enormous halo. And then, suddenly, the rope flew out over the crowd.

It darted as true and swift as an arrow. The loop fell over the head of the Badlands Kid. Before the outlaw could reach his guns, the sheriff pulled back sharply. The loop tightened over the Kid's chest and pinned his arms in tight. His horse shied and threw him to the ground. The sheriff pulled him in, like a man with a fish on the end of the line.

"Take his guns, boys," the sheriff said. "This here is the Badlands Kid. And it looks like the Sphinx has won himself the reward money."

CHAPTER 12

The show was over. The outlaw was locked in jail, and the Saturday night crowd headed for home in buggies and spring wagons. It was quite a show, folks agreed, that featured the capture of a notorious badman.

But Pa's chiming watch would never again strike the hour. It was a thing of dangling springs and broken hands. In that sudden moment when the outlaw's horse threw him, the watch had fallen to the ground. An iron horseshoe had split it open. Jane and Paul found it in the dust, and the sheriff gathered it up as evidence to send back to Cactus City. It would link the Badlands Kid to the holdup of Jeb Grimes.

Later the sheriff returned to the wagon, with a fresh piece of straw between his teeth.

"Hello, Sheriff," Mama smiled. "You're just in time for a cup of coffee."

"Thank you, ma'am."

"It looks like you'll win the election, broken leg and

all," Pa said. "Now that you captured the Badlands Kid."

"It'll help my chances. We'll know election day."

But Mr. Mysterious & Company would be long gone by election day. They might never know how things turned out.

"Mister Sphinx," the sheriff grinned. "You gave me information leading to the capture of the Badlands Kid. Here's your fifty dollars reward money. I deducted it from them gold pieces of Jeb Grimes's that the Kid buried."

"Thank you, sir," Paul said.

"What you going to spend it on?"

Paul was noncommittal. "Things," he said. But he had already talked it over with Jane and Anne and sworn them to secrecy. They would buy Pa a new watch.

"Better let me hold that money for you, before you lose it," Mama smiled. She never lost a thing—not even her temper.

"Sleeping Princess," the sheriff said. "I did enjoy your floating act. And you have right pretty hair. Just like my fiancée. She wears hers like that." And then he turned to Mama. "She's Judge Abbey's daughter over in Shotwell, New Mexico."

"We're heading that way," Pa said. "We'll be putting on our show in Shotwell."

The sheriff grinned. "Then you folks could do me a real favor."

"Name it, Sheriff," Pa said.

"Mary Jo has a birthday coming up three weeks

from Tuesday. I've got a fine two-year-old filly for her that I raised and broke myself. With the election coming up and the Badlands Kid to be tried and this broken leg of mine, I've been wondering how to get Mary Jo's present to her on time. If you could tie the filly to your wagon and take her along, I'd be much obliged."

"Done!" Pa smiled. "We'll see she gets her birthday present—on time too."

"And if you youngsters," the sheriff added, "would brush down the filly every day, I'd pay you five dollars."

"Oh, we'll brush her every day," Jane said.

"And water and graze her all she wants," Paul added.

The sheriff nodded. "Here's your five dollars in advance."

"Have another cup of coffee," Mama said.

"No, thank you, ma'am. I've got to get back to my prisoner. I'll bring the filly around before you leave town."

The show wagon remained in Dry Creek over Sunday, but early Monday morning it was on the trail. Madam Sweetpea had company at the tail gate of the wagon. The filly, whose name was Ladybelle, walked beside the family cow, and they took turns switching flies.

Together with Mama, in the rear of the wagon, the youngsters pored over their Sears, Roebuck catalog. There were dozens of watches illustrated, and finally, during school recess, they chose the one they wanted for Pa. It was a stem-winder, the newest thing in watches. Most men, if they owned a watch at all, had to wind it with a key. This one had roman numerals and hands like gold lace. And it chimed the hours. There wasn't a thing wrong with the watch—except the price.

"Sixty dollars." Paul whistled softly.

That was a fortune. But with the reward and the money for brushing down Ladybelle, they would have a total of fifty-five dollars. If they could find some way to earn another five dollars they would be able to send for Pa's watch in time for Christmas.

Every evening when Pa made camp, the youngsters brushed and curried Ladybelle from her forelock to the tip of her tail. Getting at the filly's back was a problem at first, for not even Jane could reach that high with the brush. But Paul licked the problem. He brushed Ladybelle's back—by simply standing on his stilts.

Ladybelle was a gentle, sweet-tempered chestnut, and the more the youngsters took care of her, the more they fell in love with her. Folks along the trail always stopped to admire the filly. Jane had always wanted a horse of her own, and for a few weeks, at least, it was like a dream come true.

The days went by, and it seemed to Paul that they must be in the very middle of New Mexico, at least. During schooltime Paul gazed at his *McGuffey's Third Reader,* but found his thoughts lingering on the trail ahead. Dark fell a little earlier each day and California came a little closer. One day soon their traveling life would come to an end. Paul tried not to think about it. He wished he could stay with the show wagon forever.

"Now," Mama said, "it's time for our singing lesson."

Jane and Paul snapped their books closed with such a crack that Pa, up on the wagon seat, thought he heard a pair of rifle shots. Mama sat herself at the portable piano.

"Let's warm up on the scale," she said.

The youngsters sang the scale up and down—and down and up. They all liked to sing, and there were times when Pa wished he had cotton wool to plug up his ears. Scales, he often told Mama, were for fish. He turned his head into the wagon.

"By gosh and by golly—they ought to be able to hear that screeching all the way across the line into Arizona!"

But later, when Mama was leading her students in "Listen to the Mockingbird," Pa joined in with his bull-fiddle voice. The Professor, seated near Mama's feet, began to yip. That started Ladybelle whinnying, and finally Madam Sweetpea joined in with her foghorn of a *moo-o-o-o-o-o-o*.

Jackrabbits stopped to take notice. An antelope in a clump of sage turned to look. It was a strange and bewildering sight, that gaily colored show wagon, as it lurched and creaked and poured song into the still afternoon.

Every three or four days they came to a town and there was a show to give. The wagon kept on its westward journey, leaving summer behind and entering the first days of fall.

Mama was anxious to reach Shotwell by Tuesday, for that would be Mary Jo Abbey's birthday, and it wouldn't do to be late with the sheriff's filly. All the way from Dry Creek the youngsters had kept an eye out for outlaws and road agents. Mama had put the gold pieces for Pa's watch in a straw bag, which she buried in her trunk.

"I wonder," Pa would say from time to time, "if Newt Hastings got himself re-elected sheriff. A fine young man, he is."

Every day the youngsters coached the Professor in the art of skipping rope—and he learned to do it. He got so he *liked* to jump rope, and he almost wore out the children's arms. Pa promised to let the Professor give his first show performance in Shotwell. He printed up new handbills and sent them ahead.

Extra Feature!
THE PROFESSOR
Greatest Wonder Dog in the West!
See Him Skip Rope!

On Monday afternoon—the day before Mary Jo's birthday—the show wagon was within five miles of Shotwell. Pa was whistling cheerfully, for he expected to make town that evening, when one of the wagon wheels hit a sharp rock. There came a clank and a ringing of metal and a crunch.

"Whoa, Hocus! Whoa, Pocus!"

"Andrew—what is it?" Mama called out.

Pa jumped to the ground and looked at what remained of the right front wheel. The iron rim had sprung loose and the wheel had broken against the rock. Two of the spokes hung in splinters. The wagon stood at a list, like a ship on a reef.

"Looks like this is as far as we go," Pa announced. "I'll ride into town and see if I can get us a new wheel."

School was out. Jane and Paul and Anne, together with the Professor, climbed to the ground to have a look at the damage. Pa glanced all around the trail. There were large boulders standing everywhere, and the largest towered just behind the wagon. It was as flat as the side of a barn.

"You'll be safe here," Pa said, and unhitched Hocus. "I'll be back tonight."

He got his saddle from the wagon and checked the sun. He might be able to get back before dark if he hurried. He saddled up Hocus and turned for a look at his family. They were lined up from Mama on down to the Professor—like the notes of the scale.

"Now, you young 'uns stay out of mischief," he said. "I'll be back for supper. I may be a little late, but I'll be back."

Then he mounted the saddle and headed down the trail toward town—at a gallop. He had left Mama his rifle, but he was sure she wouldn't need it.

Ten minutes later he was out of sight.

CHAPTER 13

The first thing the Hackett youngsters did was explore the big slab of rock about thirty feet away from the wagon. It had strange signs on it.

"Indian markings," Jane said. "I'll bet this is one of their superstition rocks. Full of spirits and things."

"It's kind of creepy," Paul admitted.

But the sun was still high in the sky, and not even Anne, walking about on her toes, was scared of spirits and things in the daylight. But what if Pa didn't get back before night? That huge, flat rock with its Indian markings might look fearful at night.

Mama got out the material Jane had bought for a dress. This would be a good time to get Jane started on it.

Pa rode into Shotwell around four o'clock by the sun. It was a shady town with live oaks growing along the main street. There were only a few people to be seen—even in the shade. Pa pulled up to the blacksmith shop and found the doors locked. He tied Hocus to the hitch rail and walked into the barbershop.

"Howdy," he said. "I'm looking for the blacksmith. I need a new wheel for my wagon."

The barber adjusted his green visor. "The blacksmith's in jail. The mayor and Judge Abbey, too."

Pa looked at the barber as if the man might be pulling his leg. "You mean to say the mayor and judge are in jail?"

"Shore do, stranger."

"Where will I find Miss Mary Jo Abbey?"

"I expect she's at home, like everybody else. That yeller house right across the way."

Pa crossed the street and stood on the porch of the yellow house. He knocked against the door. There was no answer. He knocked again. And again.

Finally, a young lady came to the door. She had proud, defiant eyes. "What do you want?" she asked.

"Are you Miss Mary Jo Abbey?"

"I am."

"I've just come all the way from Dry Creek. Sheriff Newt Hastings asked me to look you up."

Suddenly her face broke into smiles. "I thought you were one of the men from the Double T ranch. Please come in."

Pa stepped into a handsome parlor with fine lamps and leather chairs. "What's happening in this town?" he asked. "Is it true that your father and the mayor and even the blacksmith are in jail?"

"Yes," Miss Mary Jo nodded. "It's hardly safe to go outdoors. My father sent one of the men of the Double T ranch to state prison for cattle rustling. Today, his friends came to town, mad as hornets. They're all from the Double T ranch and not one of them any good. They shot up the street and locked my father in jail. Then they rounded up the mayor. And when our blacksmith put up some fight, they locked him up too. The sheriff is away and until he gets back—there's no telling what's going to happen."

"I'll tell you what's going to happen," Pa said. "We're going to get your father, the mayor, and the blacksmith out of jail."

Until the blacksmith was set free, Pa was thinking, there would be no buying a new wheel. And he couldn't return to the wagon without one.

"But how?" Miss Mary Jo asked. "Those ruffians in town won't let you get near the jail. They've taken it over."

"Give me a minute to think," Pa said. "I've been known to have a trick or two up my sleeve."

Pa began to pace across the room, sharpening his beard with every step. He picked up a small rock from the mantel and began bouncing it in his hand. He looked at the rock. "Is this gold ore?"

"Yes. Father brought it back from California. It's not worth very much—but it's gold."

"By gosh and by golly," Pa said. "I know just how we'll outwit those Double T critters."

At the show wagon, the Professor began to growl.

"What is it, Professor?" Jane asked.

She looked up. An Indian appeared as if from
nowhere. There was a single turkey feather tucked in
his headband. He stood at Ladybelle's rump.

Mama turned with a gasp. "What are you doing
here?" He looked like a renegade Indian, up to trouble.

Paul, who was on the other side of the wagon, drew
Pa's rifle from the boot. Anne stood stock-still on the
tips of her toes.

The Indian peered at Ladybelle. "I take horse," he
said.

"You'll do no such thing," Mama declared. "Paul!"

Paul ducked under the wagon, and Mama took the
rifle from his hands.

"Now you get," she said. "I'll count to ten, and if
you're not out of sight by then, I'll shoot."

The Indian stared down the barrel of the rifle and Mama began to count. If she was nervous, she didn't show it. She had seen many Indians in her travels, some good and some bad. This one looked all bad.

"Five," she was saying. "Six . . . seven . . . eight . . ."

The Indian was gone. He had hardly made a sound.

"Whew!" Paul breathed.

"All right," Mama said. "We'll stay close together until Pa gets back. In the wagon, all of you."

That Indian may be back, she was thinking. And he may bring friends.

Pa was sauntering along the boardwalk when he came to a rough-looking man sitting on a hitching rail.

"Good day, sir," Pa said. "That's a mighty fine blue shirt you're wearing."

The man looked up. "You loco, mister? I'm wearing a green shirt."

"It looks blue to me."

Pa kept walking and met another man, cleaning his gun on an apple box. "Howdy," Pa said. "Aren't you Tom Jennings? He has red hair just like yours."

"You must be tetched in the head," the man said. "My hair's not red."

"It looks red to me," Pa said.

Then Pa moved along to three unshaven cowhands, talking in whispers in front of the jailhouse. Miss Mary Jo had told him that the leader of the bunch wore a dirty brown hat and had a squint in one eye. His name, she said, was Ed Blackberry.

"Excuse me, gentlemen," Pa said. "I'm looking for the local jewel setter. I'm told he wears a gray hat. Ah, you sir, you're wearing a gray hat."

Ed Blackberry took off his hat and squinted at it. "Mister, your saddle is slipping. This here is a brown hat. Who are you?"

"Just a lonely wanderer," Pa said, noticing that the other men he had spoken to were coming over. He dug the lump of gold ore out of his pocket. "Found this pretty green stone, and I'm looking for a jeweler to set it in a tiepin for me."

"Green?" one of the ruffians said. "Why, that stone's not green. It's—"

Ed Blackberry kicked the man's boot to shut his mouth. "Let me see that green rock of yours," he said.

Pa handed it over. "Green as envy, sir."

Ed Blackberry squinted at the gold nugget. "Where did you say you found this stone?"

"Down in Mexico a few weeks ago."

"Were there any more *green* stones like this?"

"Why, there must be a whole mountain of it," Pa said grandly. "Of course it's not worth anything. But it's pretty to look at, isn't it? See there, how it sparkles in the sun?"

Ed Blackberry squinted at his friends and then back at Pa. "Where in Mexico?"

"About a two weeks' ride south, once you cross the Rio Grande. A little town hidden away in the mountains. Name of Zapata. A backward little spot. Why, I was the first white man they ever saw."

"And that's where you picked up this stone?"

"Why, they pave their streets with it in Zapata."

"You don't say," Ed Blackberry said.

"I do say," Pa said. "Well, good day, gentlemen."

"Just a minute, stranger," Ed Blackberry said. "Have you told anyone else about Zapata?"

"No one else has asked me."

"Keep it under your hat—understand?"

Pa smiled. "Whatever you say, my good man." And he walked away. He turned the corner and flattened himself against the building. He could hear the men from the Double T talking it over.

"I tell you that critter's color-blind. He told me my shirt was blue."

"He said my hair was red."

"And he thinks gold is green!"

"Boys," Ed Blackberry said, "there must be enough gold in Zapata to make us all rich as kings. You heard what he said. They pave the streets with it. Boys, what are we waiting for?"

"Let's ride!"

"We'll pick up our stuff at the ranch—and head for Mexico!"

In less than a minute the troublemakers were riding out of sight in a cloud of dust. As far as Pa could guess,

they would spend a lifetime looking for the golden streets of Zapata in the wilds of Mexico. Good riddance, he thought. Pa himself had never been in Mexico nor heard of a town called Zapata.

Miss Mary Jo hurried down the front steps of her house and came running across the street. She met Pa at the jail, where the keys were still hanging on the hook. In less than a minute the prisoners were set free. Judge Abbey, who wore green sleeve garters on his arms, shook one of Pa's hands, while the mayor shook the other.

"Judge," Pa said, "those are mighty fine-looking gold arm garters you're wearing."

"Gold?" the judge said. "Why, they're green, sir. Green as Mary Jo's eyes."

Then Pa explained how he had cleared the town of the men from the Double T, and everyone had a good laugh.

"Blacksmith," Pa said. "I need a new wheel for my wagon. We're broke down about five miles east of here."

"I'll not only fix you up with a new wheel," the blacksmith beamed. "I'll ride out with you and help you put it on."

It was growing dark along the trail. Paul found himself watching the spirit rock as if live Indians might jump out of it. But so far, not another Indian had turned up anywhere, and Mama was beginning to think she had frightened the stranger away.

But the sun set, and night fell, and still Pa didn't arrive. An owl hooted in the distance, and Anne turned with a whimper.

"I'm scared."

"Pa ought to be back any minute," Jane said. But she was beginning to feel a little frightened herself. Other night sounds started up, together with a moaning wind. Another owl hooted, a little nearer than the first, and a coyote began to howl on a far rock.

"It's kind of spooky," Paul admitted.

"You stop frightening yourselves," Mama said. "Pa can't be much longer."

A crescent moon was rising, but it didn't throw much light. Only enough to create strange shapes among the rocks. Another owl hooted, sending the shivers up Jane's spine. "The owls seem to be coming closer," she whispered.

Anne began to cry.

"Sh-h-h-h," Mama said. "You mustn't make a sound."

Again came the hooting of an owl, and now a shiver went up Paul's spine. "That's not an owl," he said. "That's a signal. An Indian signal. They keep getting closer!"

A jackrabbit shot through the brush and Mama cocked the rifle. But then the rabbit disappeared and a tense silence fell over the wagon.

Paul listened to the moaning wind and wished he could shut his eyes, but he didn't dare. The owls were hooting and hooting back, as if there were a war party surrounding the wagon in the night.

There *were* Indians out there. Jane was sure they had come to take Ladybelle. And maybe the gold pieces for Pa's watch! If only Pa would hurry back—

The Professor began to bark.

"I see them," Jane gasped. "There must be a dozen!"

"Indians!" Paul breathed. "Real ones!"

Mama saw them too. They were creeping through the far rocks as silently as bobcats. She lifted Pa's rifle. How could she fight off an Indian attack with a single rifle? She listened sharply to the exchange of signals— the hooting of owls. With every beat of her heart the Indians seemed to be drawing a step nearer.

Superstition Rock, she thought desperately. "Paul! Jane! Set up Pa's magic lantern."

"What?"

"Do as I say. Quickly!"

Without another word, Jane and Paul unpacked the magic lantern. They lifted off the red plush cover, and Mama told them to face the lantern toward the spirit rock.

The owls fell silent. Only the wind sounded in the darkness now, scraping through the rocks with a whistling and a moaning.

Then, suddenly, with a great shouting, the Indians made their attack. They came down out of the badlands like the wind itself—shrieking to curdle the blood. Superstition Rock rose behind the wagon in all its tall majesty.

"The lantern!" Mama said.

An instant later the slab of rock lit up as if struck by lightning. The war shouts stopped as if cut by a knife. The Indians stopped in their tracks.

The image of a great waterfall appeared in the night. It flickered, but one could almost feel the spray! And then the waterfall disappeared, and a man's face glowered under a tall hat. It was President Chester A. Arthur, looking out from the wall of rock.

But still the Indians didn't flee. They were stunned. They had never seen such magic! Spirit pictures appeared one after the other on the superstition rock. But when a Napoleon gun took shape in the flickering light, with its two great wheels and its cannon's mouth looking ready to fire—the Indians ran. They leaped over boulders and dove into sagebrush and didn't stop running until they had left the spirit rock far out of sight.

Inside the wagon, Pa's magic lantern was smoking and sputtering in a haze of kerosene fumes. Jane was changing the glass slides, while Paul focused each picture on the rock. They had run through all the pictures and were back to Niagara Falls and President Arthur.

"They're gone," Mama breathed at last. "You can put away the magic lantern."

Paul blew out the lantern wick and the spirit rock fell dark.

A few minutes later Pa rode up with the blacksmith, and Mama still had the rifle in her arms.

"Andrew," she said, with a great smile of relief, "welcome home."

Pa sniffed the kerosene fumes. "If I didn't know better I'd think you had put on a magic lantern show."

"We did!" Jane said.

And suddenly they were all talking at once, telling Pa every detail of the Indian attack.

"I declare," Pa kept saying. "I declare."

"It was the Napoleon gun that scared them off," Paul said. "I'll bet they're still running."

"I reckon they are," said the blacksmith. "As we were coming along we saw Indians scampering through the brush like jackrabbits."

CHAPTER 14

Everyone in town lined the boardwalks of Shotwell to watch the show wagon arrive. Pa waved his hat right and left, and Mama smiled in her starched white bonnet. Hocus and Pocus lifted their legs in high prancing steps, and the Professor wagged his tail in Anne's face.

The mayor was there, puffing a cigar and smiling. The blacksmith, in his leather apron, waved his big hand. And Judge Abbey, with Miss Mary Jo on his arm, stepped out in the street to stop the procession.

"Mr. Mysterious," Judge Abbey announced. "This town owes you a vote of thanks. You cleared the varmints out of here as slick as the Pied Piper of Hamelin. Welcome to Shotwell!"

A shout went up from one side of the street to the other. Pa spread his arms in a grand gesture. "It's a pleasure to be in your fine town. And to you, Miss Mary Jo—a mighty happy birthday!"

"Glory be!" Miss Mary Jo started in surprise. "How did you know?"

"Ah," Pa smiled. "Mr. Mysterious knows all, except how the election turned out back in Dry Creek."

"Newt Hastings was re-elected hands down," Judge Abbey said. "The stagecoach brought us the news."

"Joy!" Mama smiled.

"Good news, indeed," Pa said, turning to Miss Mary Jo. "That beau of yours asked us to deliver a small remembrance. If you'll just close your eyes—"

Miss Mary Jo glanced around at the townspeople lining the boardwalks and felt herself blush.

"Go ahead," Judge Abbey said. "Close your eyes."

Pa climbed down from the wagon and hurried around to the tail gate. A moment later he placed a piece of rope in her hands.

"Keep those eyes closed," he said, "and tell us what this feels like."

"It feels," Miss Mary Jo said, "like a hank of rope."

"That's mighty thoughtful of Newt Hastings to send you a piece of rope," Pa said. "What are you going to do with it?"

Miss Mary Jo, with her eyes still closed, didn't know what to think. "I've been needing a new clothesline," she said. "That's what I'll use it for."

"Open your eyes," Pa grinned.

Miss Mary Jo's long lashes parted. She looked at the rope in her hand and then followed it along to the other end. And that was when she saw Ladybelle. As she looked at the filly, tears of joy came to her eyes and she rushed forward. She threw her arms around Ladybelle's neck and looked as happy as it was possible for a young lady of nineteen to look—which is very happy indeed. "How beautiful you are," she said to the filly, and then she smiled up at Jane and Paul and Anne. "Does she have a name?"

"Ladybelle," they answered in a chorus of three voices.

"Ladybelle," Miss Mary Jo murmured. "What a lovely name."

"We brushed her every day," Anne piped up. "Just like the sheriff told us to."

Miss Mary Jo rubbed Ladybelle's nose. "Why, I never saw such a well-brushed horse," she said. "Brushed and curried and shiny as satin."

"Now that the sheriff has been re-elected," Mama said to Miss Mary Jo, "I expect you two will be setting the date."

"We've already set it," Miss Mary Jo said. "Newt and I are going to be married on the first day of December!"

"Folks," Judge Abbey said to Pa and Mama and the youngsters, "there are eats at our house and we've been waiting for you. You must be hungry, so come along."

Later that afternoon, the youngsters tried to figure out some way of earning the extra money they needed for Pa's watch.

"Maybe I could sweep out the barbershop," Paul said. "The barber might give me a nickel."

Mama turned to Jane. "I think I heard Judge Abbey say that Mrs. Becker's daughter is sick in bed. She's just your age."

"Maybe I can read to her," Jane said.

"I'll find something and sell it," Anne said.

But the afternoon didn't work out quite as expected. The barber told Paul that he hadn't cut anyone's hair in a week and so there was nothing to sweep up. Jane cut across a vacant lot to the Becker house, but Trudy Becker wasn't sick. It was her brother Roger who was in bed, and he didn't want to be read to at all. He had poison ivy.

Jane quickly made friends with Trudy and her sister Sharon, who were planning a taffy pull for the next afternoon.

"Can you come, Jane?" Trudy asked eagerly. "You'll meet all the girls in town."

"It'll be loads of fun," Sharon added.

"I'd like to," Jane said wistfully, "but—"

"Please come."

"But we'll be leaving in the morning."

"Maybe you can stay," Trudy said. "Just until tomorrow."

Jane tried not to show the flush of excitement she felt. She didn't want her new friends to know that with the show wagon always on the move, she had never had time for a real party. "I'll ask Pa," she said.

The girls spent the whole afternoon chattering away—about school, about the party, and about nothing at all. If only, if only, Jane thought—if only Pa would stay an extra day!

Meanwhile, Anne busied herself trying to earn money for Pa's watch. She caught a pair of fat frogs not far from the wagon. She offered them for sale at two for a nickel, but no one bought them. When night drew near it was easy enough to figure out why. A croaking started up from one end of Shotwell to the other. It sounded to Anne as if there were more frogs in town than people.

That night, during the show, Pa could hardly make himself heard over the croaking of frogs.

"Ladies and (*croak*) gentlemen," he said from the footlights. "Boys and (*croak*) girls, and girls and (*croak*) boys. We present for your (*croak*) amusement (*croak*), edification, and (*croak-croak-croak*) jollification our traveling (*croak*) temple of (*croak*) mysteries! A program of (*croak-croak-croak-croak*) wonders and (*croak*) marvels! Feats of (*croak*) legerdemain and (*croak-croak-croak*) tricks of prestidigitation!"

Mama had told Anne to set her two frogs free.

"But I want to keep them," Anne protested. "They like to be petted."

"We don't need any frogs in the show," Mama said. "We've got two horses, a cow, and a dog—not to mention Pa's rabbits. No, thank you. Set those frogs loose."

"Please, Mama."

"They go *out*."

But now, as Mama was striking chords on the piano—the piano croaked. Joy! she thought. It was as if she were playing *croaks* instead of *chords*.

When she lifted the top of the piano—out jumped Anne's fat frogs. They disappeared into the shadows.

"Anne!" Mama whispered. "I told you to set your frogs loose!"

"I did!" Anne insisted. "Those are different ones."

"Find them before they get into Pa's props."

But in the darkness at the side of the stage, the frogs were nowhere to be found. One of them turned up a moment later when Jane handed Pa a trick box.

"Empty," Pa said to the crowd.

Out leaped a fat frog.

Pa was more surprised than his audience. The folks took it to be part of the trick.

And later, when he pulled a rabbit out of a hat—out came a frog as well. When he picked up a tube, up popped a frog. While Paul was hidden away in the Sphinx table, he felt a frog in his pants leg. When Jane was floating in the air, a frog leaped on the sofa and Jane almost floated down on him. The crowd laughed every time a frog appeared. They thought Mr. Mysterious had planned it all.

But backstage, Mama and Jane and Paul hunted frogs in every shadow.

"I told you to set your frogs loose before the show," Mama whispered to Anne. "They're getting in everything! You're due for a spanking, Anne Hackett."

"I *did* turn them free," Anne insisted.

"You hid them in the piano."

"Those were *different* frogs!" Anne said.

"Mama," Jane said. "It sounds like a dozen of 'em croaking back here."

"It's not a dozen," Anne said. "It's only ten."

"Ten!" Mama gasped.

Anne nodded. "You only told me to set two frogs loose. You didn't tell me I couldn't catch any more."

"Anne Hackett!"

"Abracadabra Day!" Anne said.

Mama opened her mouth, but not a word came out. Paul snickered and Jane smiled.

At the footlights, Pa turned a potato into a frog—much to his own surprise.

"Mr. Mysterious," Judge Abbey called. "You could do us a favor by turning all our frogs into potatoes."

"That would take me all of a year," Pa smiled, "and we're due in California by Christmas. Can't spare the time, Judge."

Finally Pa introduced the Professor.

"The Wonder Dog of the West," he said, "making his premier appearance in your fine city of Shotwell. He's part dog and part frog. Watch him jump!"

Jane and Paul came on stage and began swinging the rope. At a signal, Anne let go of the Professor. He leaped toward the kerosene footlights and skipped rope with all four legs. The crowd was astonished. Then the Professor stood on his hind legs and jumped. The townspeople burst into applause. The Wonder Dog of the West skipped

rope at least ten times and would have been happy to
skip rope until midnight. A huge frog leaped onstage,
and when the rope came down it leaped.

"A dog and a frog jumping rope!" a man yelled out in
utter amazement. "I never seen anything like that in all
my born days!"

Later that night, after the crowd had gone and the
wagon was packed, Pa kept a lantern lit and unfolded
his map on the ground.

"Pa," Jane said hesitantly.

"Look here," he smiled, placing a finger on the map. "We'll be across the Arizona line in another week. And way over here—there's the Pacific Ocean. We'll be looking at it Christmas Day. But we'll have to hurry."

"Pa, I've been invited to a party."

He looked up suddenly and met Jane's eyes. "A party?"

"A taffy pull."

The lantern lit up Jane's face. Her hair, already brushed out for the night, fell below her shoulders. She had waited until the last moment to tell Pa about the party, and now she felt her heart skipping a beat.

"Well, now," Pa said gently. "That's splendid. When is it?"

"Tomorrow. Tomorrow afternoon."

Pa glanced down at his map. His eye followed the trail west. San Diego was still a long way off, and Christmas was coming closer every day.

"Why, I can't think of anything more fun than a taffy pull." But still he peered at the map in the lamplight. With Madam Sweetpea slowing the wagon down, it already looked like a race against the calendar.

Jane felt the tears rising. She knew she was asking the impossible. "Can I go, Pa? Can I?"

Pa hesitated only another moment.

"Of course you can," he said.

Jane caught her breath in sheer surprise. "You mean it, Pa? You mean we can stay over?"

"If your mind's made up to go to that party, you're going to go." He folded up the map. "Now it's time you were in bed, young 'un."

But Jane found herself rooted to the spot. She watched Pa blow out the lantern and hook it on the side of the wagon. He began to whistle "Buckeye Jim." Her heart began skipping beats again.

"Pa?"

"We won't stand here all night talking about it. You're going to that party."

"But it might make us late for Christmas dinner with Uncle Fred and Aunt Emma."

"We'll get there somehow."

"It's just a taffy pull."

"There's nothing more fun than a taffy pull."

"Maybe I'll be invited to parties when we settle down in California."

"No doubt. But don't you go changing your mind. We're staying over here in Shotwell."

Jane was glad Pa had blown out the lantern. She was glad for the darkness, for she could feel the tears again in her eyes. "I haven't changed my mind."

"That's fine."

"I never exactly made it up."

"It sounded made up to me."

"It looks to me, Pa," she said, "if we're going to California we ought to get along."

"No doubt. But a day won't matter."

"Yes it will."

"Now you get along to bed."

"Do you really think we can cross the Arizona line in a week, Pa?"

There was a still moment. She could almost see the smile spread across Pa's face. And then he hugged her close, picking her up off the ground. "I can feel your heart breaking, child. But by gosh and by golly, you've got spirit. You're a regular young lady and I'm proud of you. Parties? Why, in California you'll get so many invites you won't know which way to turn. Now give me a kiss and get to bed."

The next morning, an hour after sunup, the show wagon headed west along the main street of Shotwell. Trudy and Sharon Becker came out on their front porch to watch the wagon go by. Jane waved. The girls waved back. And soon they were out of sight of each other. What a silly goose she had been, Jane thought. Why, soon she would have so many invites she wouldn't know which way to turn.

CHAPTER
15

One day was like the next, and yet every day was different. Mr. Mysterious & Company encountered new adventures, sometimes twice a day, and created excitement in every town they passed through.

In a week to the day, they crossed the line into Arizona Territory.

Along the trail they met strange and wonderful travelers. They shared their noon meal once with a man pushing all his belongings in a large wheelbarrow. The next night the show wagon camped with a family from Iowa. Their name was Caxton, and they had brought along their beehives. Six hives were lashed to the side of their wagon, and the bees had no trouble keeping up with their traveling home. But Paul, forgetting that he had already had his Abracadabra Day, rapped the hives with a stick to stir up the bees. Everyone ran for cover, and Paul got a spanking.

By early November the Hackett children had earned only $1.65 doing odd jobs in the towns they visited.

They had to be careful not to let Pa know what they were up to. Even then they wondered how they would ever save enough for Pa's watch.

The towns in Arizona seemed even farther apart than they had in New Mexico and Texas. Meanwhile, the youngsters spent their days in the wagon school, and in her spare time Jane, with Mama's help, worked on her new dress—she wanted to wear it Christmas Day. The Professor spent long hours on the wagon seat beside Pa.

It was Tuesday, with not a show town in sight. The trail was strewn with rocks and the wagon lurched and shook. Suddenly Mama's voice rang out in exasperation.

"Andrew! Stop this wagon. Stop this instant!"

Pa leaned back on the reins and the Professor leaped to his feet. What had happened? Pa could hardly remember the last time Mama had lost her temper. He glanced quickly inside the wagon. Had Paul made Madam Sweetpea disappear again?

Mama stood with a needle in one hand and a length of thread in the other. Her eyes, always so gentle, flashed like summer lightning.

"Andrew," she said. "It seems like I've spent an hour trying to thread this needle for sister. The way this wagon is churning she'll never get her dress made."

"The trail is a mite uneven," Pa said, smiling now. "Go ahead and thread your needle."

Mama sharpened the point of the thread and slipped it through the needle's eye. She gave a sigh of relief.

"Git up, Hocus," Pa said. "Git up, Pocus."

But after that, when the trail was rough, Pa sometimes had to stop twice an hour for needle threading. Mama had always wanted a sewing machine, but there was no room in the wagon—what with the magic props, the trunk, and the portable piano.

On the following Friday, at noon, Pa gathered the youngsters together.

"Who can keep a secret the best?" he whispered.

"I can!" Anne said.

"I can!" Paul said.

"I can!" Jane said.

Pa gave them each a little wink as if to seal the bargain. "We'll be getting into Broken Jaw tomorrow. It seems to me we ought to send for a sewing machine. It could be waiting for Mama in San Diego on Christmas Day."

"Oh yes!" Jane said. "She would love it!"

"Not a word, now. Not a peep."

The youngsters nodded, and Jane smiled to herself. That made *two* secrets to be kept—Mama's sewing machine and Pa's watch.

The town of Broken Jaw stood on the empty desert like a ship at sea. The show wagon arrived late, and Pa barely had time to slip away to send for Mama's sewing machine. Paul earned a nickel toward the watch money by renting out his stilts to one of the town boys. Standing on them during the show, the boy could see over everyone's head.

But if night had brought on all the frogs in Shotwell, New Mexico, it seemed as if every mosquito in the Arizona Territory came to the magic show in Broken Jaw. Pa had to beat them off with his wand, and Jane was bitten while floating in mid-air. The show wagon got out of Broken Jaw as soon as it could—and that wasn't fast enough to suit Mama.

But it seemed to Pa, as he crossed out the days on the calendar, that Madam Sweetpea was dragging her feet more than usual. The end of November approached, and still the California line was nowhere in sight.

"We could count a handkerchief," Paul said, "and measure how fast we're traveling."

It would be more fun counting a handkerchief than studying his *McGuffey's Reader*.

"All right," Mama said. "We'll make it our arithmetic lesson for the day."

After the noon meal Paul tied a handkerchief to the rear wheel, and Mama set her kitchen hourglass. Between them, Jane and Paul took turns counting the handkerchief every time it went around. It made a dreamy kind of schoolwork. The wheel turned slowly, and Paul found himself thinking about San Diego and the cattle ranch. Why did Mama want windows with curtains, only to look out on the same thing every day? Why did Jane have to have school friends and parties?

Why couldn't they just go on traveling from town to town entertaining folks? But soon he would have to put away his blue uniform with its shiny brass buttons, and

Pa would lay aside his magic wand and the kerosene footlights. If only Pa would change his mind! But it was no use. Once Pa made up his mind, it stayed made.

At the end of the hour, by Mama's sandglass, the handkerchief had gone around 492 times.

"Now," Mama said, "let's see how far we travel each hour."

The wheel stood three feet tall. Jane figured out that the wheel spanned just under 9½ feet every time it went around. By multiplying the circumference by the number of times the handkerchief popped in view, Jane learned that the wagon traveled a little less than 4674 feet per hour.

"But that ain't even a mile," Paul said. "A mile is 5280 feet."

"Then if we travel ten hours," Jane said, "we're not covering ten miles a day at all!"

Quiet alarm appeared in Mama's eyes. If Jane's figures were correct, it meant the show wagon was doing less than *nine* miles a day. And if that were true—they wouldn't make Uncle Fred's ranch in San Diego for Christmas Day.

Mama worked the figures for herself. There wasn't a mistake to be found. She showed them to Pa, up on the wagon seat.

"That lazy, ornery cow," Pa grimaced. "Nine miles a day, is it?"

Pa thought about it for two days, but there was no way to move Madam Sweetpea along any faster than she wanted to go. Pa even bought an old straw hat from an Indian squaw and tied it to the wagon gate. Fond as Madam Sweetpea was of straw hats, and even with this one dangling a few feet in front of her nose, the cow wouldn't hurry a single step.

On some days, Pa drove the team an extra hour. But on other days the wind came up, and the rain. On the first of December the show wagon was still in Arizona Territory—stuck fast in the mud.

"This is the day Newt Hastings and Mary Jo Abbey set for their wedding, way back in Shotwell," Mama said.

"By gosh and by golly, we'll celebrate," Pa declared.

And celebrate Mr. Mysterious & Company did. Mama fixed a fine supper inside the wagon, and they ate with the wind whipping the canvas and rain leaking into pans Mama set about the floor.

A week later, on a clear winter day, the show wagon crossed the California line.

"San Diego," Pa announced. "It's out there somewhere!"

And Mama said, "The first one to see the Pacific Ocean gets an extra Christmas dumpling!"

Anne peeled her eyes at once, even though it was eighteen days to Christmas and all of California had yet to be crossed.

Sand dunes stretched as far as the eye could see, and it took three days to get through them. The show wagon kept getting stuck in the loose sand until Pa found two old planks of wood. He would set them in front of the wheels where the sand looked treacherous.

All the while time was passing, and an awful feeling came over Jane that the wagon might not make San Diego in time.

But still they pushed on. If a town stood a mile off the trail Pa wouldn't detour to play in it. A promise was a promise, and he didn't intend to disappoint his family. A week passed, and it seemed as if the Pacific Ocean would never turn up on the horizon.

But mountains did turn up. Tall and blue, like a barrier in the distance. Paul watched the mountains grow closer and closer day by day. Hocus and Pocus might still be trying to haul the wagon over the high passes by the Fourth of July.

Meanwhile, Jane worried about her new dress. Even though Mama helped her, she didn't see how she could have it finished by Christmas. But Mama finally got it pinned up in a fitting, taking tucks here and there, while the wagon rattled and shook. The pins attacked Jane like a swarm of Broken Jaw mosquitoes.

"Ouch!"

"Hold still, sister."

"Ouch!"

The wagon was already in the foothills, lurching and swaying over the trail. Mama finished the fitting and Jane breathed again.

But the trail ahead looked even worse. It climbed—and with every mile the wagon slowed. Pa stopped near a ranch house. He was gone almost an hour and returned with a smile and a brace of horses. He had bought them to help Hocus and Pocus pull the show wagon over the mountains.

On the twenty-first day of December, Mr. Mysterious & Company were camped high in the mountains. And still the Pacific Ocean was nowhere on the horizon. Paul climbed a tree and looked as far west as he could, but there was not a drop of water to be seen except in the water barrel.

The next morning, with only three days left, Pa awoke with a grin. When the family gathered around the breakfast fire, he sharpened his beard and looked slyly at each member of his family.

"We seem to have a problem," he said. "Madam Sweetpea must be the slowest cow on the face of the earth. It looks like she's going to make us late for Christmas, doesn't it?"

Mama nodded. "But you're not going to sell her, Andrew. If that's what you're thinking."

"The thought has crossed my mind."

"Pa!" Jane said with surprised horror. Mean and ornery as their cow was, Jane loved Madam Sweetpea.

"We'll be in San Diego on time," Pa declared. "—And Madam Sweetpea with us. Watch and behold!"

He let down the tail gate and propped the two planks of wood to make a runway. Then he coaxed, shoved, and pulled Madam Sweetpea up *into* the wagon.

"This lazy cow is going to *ride* to the Pacific Ocean!" Pa said. "With a team of four horses I figure we can cover twenty miles a day at least!"

Mama didn't like having a cow in the wagon, chewing everything in sight, but she didn't argue.

Madam Sweetpea was delighted. She switched her tail and mooed and looked as haughty as a queen. All that day, and the next, as travelers passed one way or the other, strange expressions turned up on their faces.

"Glory be," they were apt to say. "I swear I saw a cow in that wagon."

CHAPTER 16

It was hard to say who saw the Pacific Ocean first. The show wagon, still wet with morning dew, came around a hump of granite, and there it was through the pine trees—a shimmer of blue in the December sun.

"Behold!" Pa said in awe.

It was indeed a marvel to behold. Neither Jane nor Paul nor Anne had ever seen anything but rivers, lakes, and water holes. They had spent their lives in the Midwest, where an ocean seemed as distant and remote as China.

And now it stretched out before their eyes—on Christmas Day.

"Joy," Mama said, fixing her sunbonnet. "What a Christmas present that makes."

And Paul began putting on his shoes, even without being told.

Pa cracked the whip over his team of four horses and followed the stage road toward San Diego at the

edge of the bay. Soon they could make out sailing ships in the harbor and sea gulls floating in the wind like bits of paper.

It was just after noon when the show wagon raised a storm of dust across a mesa overlooking the bay. Grazing cattle stopped to look at the red canvas and spinning gold wheels. Jackrabbits scattered in every direction. A white ranch house stood dead ahead in the shade of a huge pepper tree. As the wagon pulled up, out burst Uncle Fred and Aunt Emma. Pa pulled back on the reins.

"You made it!" Uncle Fred shouted, whipping off his hat in sheer joy. "You made it!"

"Merry Christmas!"

It was a great reunion, full of shouts and smiles and laughter. Uncle Fred, whose eyebrows were as red as Pa's beard, helped Jane to the ground with one arm and Anne with the other.

"What fine young ladies," he beamed. "And how you've grown!"

"The Christmas table is set and waiting," Aunt Emma said.

"And this young man," said Uncle Fred, lifting his eyebrows at Paul. "This can't be Paul?"

"Yes, sir," Paul said.

"Why, the last time I saw you, you could walk under a kitchen table with room to spare. Now look at you!"

"Glory be," Aunt Emma said suddenly. "Is that a cow in the wagon?"

"It sure is!" Pa laughed, and then he explained how the show wagon had made it to the ranch in time.

"I declare," Uncle Fred said, whipping off his hat again. "That beats all."

They let down the tail gate and fixed the wooden planks to put Madam Sweetpea out to graze. But the moment Jane and Paul and Anne saw her, they froze like three wooden Indians.

Madam Sweetpea was chewing down the last of Mama's straw bag!

"Mama!" Anne grasped. "Madam Sweetpea got into your trunk!"

"It must have popped open on a bump!" Paul said.

"Pa's watch money," Jane breathed fearfully, for she knew that Madam Sweetpea didn't mind eating nails and bits of metal.

Mama quickly got the youngsters aside. "That old straw bag didn't amount to much," she said, "and Madam Sweetpea ought to be entitled to an Abracadabra Day, too."

Had Mama forgotten?

"The money for Pa's watch," Paul whispered. "You put it in the bag."

"And took it out again," Mama said. "Now don't you worry. I've been planning a special Christmas surprise for you young 'uns."

"But—"

"Wait and see."

They didn't have long to wait. Once inside the ranch house, where the table was set for a feast, Uncle Fred showed a pile of packages waiting for the Hackett family.

"Dinner can wait," Aunt Emma announced. "We're dying to know what's in these packages ourselves."

The smallest package of all was for Pa. He shook it gently and then carefully undid the wrappings.

It was a watch.

A watch that chimed the hours. A stem-winder!

"By gosh and by golly," he said reverently. "By gosh and by golly."

But Pa was no more surprised than Jane and Paul and Anne—and no more delighted. To them, it seemed the greatest Christmas surprise of all.

"But how—" Jane turned to Mama.

"I sent for it in Broken Jaw," Mama said. "I was afraid if we waited any longer, the watch wouldn't arrive in time."

"But we didn't have enough money," Paul said.

"I've been saving for a sewing machine," Mama said. "So I just used some of that money for you. Now, with the extra money you've earned—why, you can get Pa a chain to go with his new watch."

"Yes," Jane smiled. "We forgot all about the chain. Of course!"

Among Anne's packages was a rubber ball and a wonderful doll, with real hair, that Aunt Emma had made. She had made Jane a purse, with hundreds of small beads sewn on it, and Uncle Fred picked out a jackknife for Paul. One surprise followed another, with still the largest package yet to go. And that was for Mama.

When she opened the wrappings and saw the new treadle sewing machine, she was stunned. Tears sprang to her eyes. "Joy," she said. "Joy."

She hugged Pa and Jane and Paul and Anne and even the Professor. And then she hugged Uncle Fred and Aunt Emma for good measure.

"I never saw such a Christmas," she said. "And not even snow on the ground, and the sky as blue as a robin's egg."

There was just time for Jane to change into her new dress before Christmas dinner. Uncle Fred asked if she had sent all the way to Paris for it. Jane had never felt more beautiful. If there had been moments when Paul never wanted to see California, he forgot them in all the excitement.

When Uncle Fred told Pa about a piece of empty cattle land nearby, with a swimming hole on it where a boy could play hooky from school, Paul began to think settling down might be tolerable. Fun, even. When he wasn't in the swimming hole, he thought, he could still practice untying knots with his toes and palming things and grow up to be a magician like Pa.

Mama could hardly wait to get at her new sewing machine.

Pa's watch struck the hour as Uncle Fred carried in the turkey on a silver platter. "What time is the magic performance going to be?" Uncle Fred asked.

"What performance?" said Pa.

"Why, Mr. Mysterious and Company."

Pa shook his head. "Our show days are over. I'm putting away the magic wand."

Uncle Fred started carving the turkey. "Then you're going to disappoint a mighty big crowd. Soon as I mentioned we expected a magician at our place for Christmas—why, word bounced from one end of San Diego to the other. By nightfall the buggies and wagons will start arriving, and we can't turn them away without a show."

Pa sharpened his beard and glanced at Mama. "In that case, he smiled, "we'll be happy to put on a farewell performance."

The buggies and wagons, loaded with youngsters, began to arrive on the mesa at sundown. And even after it grew dark the buggies continued to gather. It was a balmy December evening, almost like summer, and the ladies hardly needed their shawls. Within ten minutes Jane had made friends with another girl her own age. And by the time the show was ready to start she had been invited to one birthday party, one taffy pull, and one sewing bee.

Pa had moved the show wagon under the giant pepper tree, and now he lit the kerosene footlights. If this was going to be his last performance, he was going to make it his best. Mama struck a chord on the piano. Then Pa sharpened his beard and stepped onto the stage. The show was under way.

Pa made his introductory remarks and called for his magic stick. Paul tripped bringing it out, to the general merriment of the crowd. Jane, in her new Christmas dress, floated in mid-air, and the Professor skipped rope. The Sphinx wriggled his nose and answered three questions.

At the piano, Mama watched Pa with a great gentleness in her eyes. He was sharpening his magician's beard for the last time. He got such joy from entertaining folks. She knew he was hurting inside, and yet he smiled in the glow of the footlights and kept a twinkle in his eye. Mama cried softly for a moment, but no one noticed except the Professor, who lifted his ears. Much as she wanted a regular schooling for the youngsters and window curtains for herself, she wished that Pa could go on polishing the black magic wand on his sleeve and pulling rabbits out of hats. But he had decided long ago to settle the family in one spot, and there was no changing his mind.

"And now the grand finale," Pa was saying. "Watch and behold! The Enchanted Dollhouse."

Jane and Paul separated the small front curtains to reveal a brightly painted playhouse in the center of the wagon stage. Pa opened its doors to show that the house was empty. Mama, at the piano, went into a light waltz. Pa picked up Anne's rag doll, with the fixed smile, and did a small dance step with it. Then he set the doll inside the playhouse and polished his magic stick on the sleeve of his coat.

"Watch and behold!"

He made a pass over the dollhouse. Mama struck a chord. And then, as if the doll had come to life, the walls of the house burst open.

And out popped Anne on her tiptoes!

The crowd gaped. Before their eyes Pa had changed a rag doll into a real girl with a real smile. Anne spread her skirt and curtsied at the footlights. Applause broke out that could almost be heard aboard the ships in the harbor.

And the show was over.

Pa blew out the footlights, and one by one the wagons and buggies turned for home. The family began packing away the magic props with an air of gloom. Paul unbuttoned his blue uniform. He was outgrowing it anyway, he thought glumly. Jane found herself gazing at the velvet couch. She would never again float in mid-air. She realized, suddenly, what fun it was to float in mid-air, and a small cry escaped her lips. The Professor pricked up his ears again.

Pa didn't say a word, and the next morning at breakfast he failed to sharpen his beard. Mr. Mysterious & Company was no more. They were simply Mr. and Mrs. Andrew Hackett and children.

"I'll drive you out to look at that homestead land," Uncle Fred said. "Why, the grass is a foot high and just waiting for cattle to graze on it."

Uncle Fred hitched up his surrey, and an hour later the Hacketts were standing in the green grass. Their gloom lifted. The blue harbor sparkled to the west. Mama picked out the spot where she wanted the house to be. The youngsters went exploring for the swimming hole, and the Professor cornered a horned toad.

Pa peered all around. In his mind's eye he could see five hundred head of cattle grazing on his land—to start, at least. "By gosh and by golly," he declared. "We'll file on it."

He filed at the county courthouse that afternoon. There was a bustling spirit to the town and a great coming and going of wagons and buggies around the plaza. New houses seemed to be going up everywhere. There was a fine hotel and a department store and no end of things to look at. Jane's eyes shone with the excitement of it all, and even Paul was a little dazzled. They stopped in a jewelry store and picked out a heavy chain for Pa's new watch. The day seemed complete.

But when they returned to Uncle Fred's ranch, a gentleman with side whiskers and a tall hat was waiting in a buggy under the shade of the pepper tree.

"Why, it's Big Jim Norton," Uncle Fred said.

The gentleman tipped his hat to the ladies. He chomped on a cigar and wore a diamond stickpin in his tie. He looked to Jane almost as important at President Chester A. Arthur.

"Mr. Mysterious," Big Jim Norton said, "I've been hearing all about the magic show you put on last night. Mighty fine, I hear. Mighty fine. How long do you expect to be in these parts?"

"That was our farewell performance," Pa said. "Our show days are over. We're staying put."

"Is that so?"

"I filed on a homestead not an hour ago."

Big Jim Norton lifted his eyebrows. "Splendid," he said.

Paul studied the man and wondered what he was up to.

"In that case," Big Jim Norton said, "we can do business."

"What business?" Pa asked.

"This is an up-and-coming town. Getting to be a regular city. Folks are coming in by the wagonload and on every ship. New faces every day. I'm building a theater, and there's nothing like a magic show to entertain folks. Why, you could put on your show once a month and we'd still have to turn folks away. Is it a bargain?" Big Jim Norton held out his hand. "All I need is a handshake."

Pa, who had spent his years amazing others, stood amazed himself. He glanced at Mama and then at the youngsters. Jane held her breath. Paul gazed up at Pa, his eyes never wider. Anne clutched the rag doll.

Pa stuck out his hand. "By gosh and by golly," he smiled. "It's a bargain. Why, we could declare it a kind of Abracadabra Day. Once a month—magic for everyone."

The two men shook hands, and Pa's watch chimed the hour. Mr. Mysterious & Company broke into smiles, and for the first time that day Pa sharpened his beard.